A THIRSTY EVIL

BOOKS BY

P. M. HUBBARD

P. M. HUBBARD

A THIRSTY EVIL

NEW YORK

ATHENEUM

1974

To
Farid and Rippu Riaz, of Chak Sandhe Khan and Lahore,
With love.

"Our natures do pursue,
Like rats that ravin down their proper bane,
A thirsty evil; and when we drink, we die."

Measure for Measure

CHAPTER ONE

I sat opposite her in a train for a couple of hours, and we neither of us said a word to each other the whole time. She was the only woman I have ever really wanted. For the matter of that, she still is. I suppose she may always be. I hope not, because it does not seem to be much good now. But I do not like the look of things.

When the train got in, I simply let her go. I had to. I have not got any of the approved opening gambits, and you cannot just tell someone that she is the only person you have ever really wanted. At least, I suppose you could, if you were drunk enough or had that sort of nerve, but I doubt, even so, whether it would be very convincing. Someone was there to meet her, an older woman. It could have been her mother, but I did not think so, and I know now that it was not. The woman who came to meet her was in excellent taste, just as her own clothes and baggage were in excellent taste. There was nothing wrong with her at all that I could see. They got a porter without any trouble, or perhaps the older woman had got him before the train came in, and the three of them went off together through the barrier. I took my cases out and followed them, but by the time I was through, I could not see her anywhere, and I just went on where I was going. That could have been the end of it, but in fact it was only the beginning.

By rights it should have been the end, because it was

all the world to a brass farthing that I should never see her again, and I did not look for her. I did not know how to set about it, and I am not the sort of man who puts advertisements in the paper, or not that sort of advertisement. I dislike cliches intensely. It was pure chance that I did see her again. Even that might not have mattered, only she recognised me. Something must have got through to her, even in the train. She did not smile, not quite, but she looked at me with a sort of slightly amused curiosity. I do not know how I looked at her, I suppose the same way I had looked at her in the train, because I still felt the same about her. She was with a man this time, not her husband, because she wore no ring, but certainly not a relation. He was different in every sort of way. I did not like the look of him at all.

We were at a publisher's party, but that did not mean a thing. You see all sorts of people at publishers' parties. She might not have anything even remotely to do with books. She certainly did not look like a writer, or not like a writer at a publisher's party. She was not playing any sort of part at all, just being mildly amused. Now that I could watch her, it occurred to me that she might have looked at me like that merely because I was part of the party. All the same, I was certain that she had recognised me. I thought she had probably just come along with the man she was with. He could be a writer. He looked capable of anything. There was no doubt she was with him. She did not seem to know anybody else. She moved round with him, talking to whoever he talked to, but not talking much to anyone. He talked all the time.

I watched the men she talked to, wondering whether they felt the same about her as I did. I did not think on the whole they did. She was not at all the standard centre of excitement. There was a quality of peace in her, and peace does not go down big at a party, least of all a publisher's party. I wanted desperately to hear her voice, but it was next to impossible to hear what anyone said, let alone the way they said it.

I got hold of Penelope and asked her who the man was. She looked worried for a moment, because it was her job to know who people were. Then she said, 'Oh, I know. A man called Canning. Friend of Alastair's.' Alastair was one of her bosses, but it is all Christian names in publishing.

I said, 'What does he do? Write?'

She looked doubtful again, but shook her head. 'I don't think so,' she said. 'He's not one of ours, anyway.'

'Who's the woman with him, then?'

She made no bones about this at all. 'Haven't the faintest idea,' she said. 'Just someone he brought with him.' The thing was, she was not particularly interested either, and it did not seem to occur to her that I should be. Nobody seemed to see what I saw. If it had been an obvious man-trap, Penelope would have known all about her by now and probably offered to introduce me. As it was, I just nodded, and Penelope darted off to tell somebody else whatever it was they wanted to know. She was a busy little woman, and a mine of information.

I circulated cautiously in their direction. I knew I might not be able to get into the conversation. I did not think Mr Canning was a man to waste words on anyone he did not know. But at least I might get near enough to hear her talk, when she did talk. The peak of the party was past, and the noise was a bit less deafening now. I had not got far when I knew she had seen me coming. As I say, she was no man-trap, but she did not miss much. Every now and then we looked at each other, just for a moment, and then the amusement went out of her face. What replaced it was not hostility, but a sort of gentle speculation. Everything she did was gentle, as if the peace inside her left no need for violence.

When I was quite close to them, Mr Canning button-

9

holed David Stringer. I did not know David well, but we did know each other, and I moved up on the other side of him. I could hear Mr Canning very clearly now, and his voice went with the rest of him. It was quick and confident and penetrating, and he asked questions all the time. I wondered if he was a lawyer of some sort. He was asking David about money. Writers think about money almost the whole time, and when they talk among themselves, that is what they talk about mostly, but they do not like coming across with figures. If they are asked questions, they become vague and if necessary evasive. David was being evasive now. Anyone would be with Mr Canning, the more so as he would not be an easy man to evade. I thought if he was a lawyer, he would be a barrister, not a solicitor.

Unless it is a meeting of souls, a conversation at this sort of party has a fairly fixed life-cycle. There is always the moment when one person or the other takes his eyes away from the person he is talking to and looks round the room to see what else is on offer. The thing is to do it first, but not too obviously. It is disconcerting to catch the other person doing it. It did not take David long to reach this point with Mr Canning, and he did not take much trouble to conceal it. Mr Canning would not be strong on the sensibilities, his own or other people's. David was a good deal taller than Mr Canning, and was talking down to him, at least in a physical sense, but now he lifted his head, quite deliberately, and looked round him, and the first eye he caught was mine. As I say, we did not know each other well, but his face lit up as if I owed him a fiver. His motives were purely selfish, of course. It could not occur to him that I actually wanted to meet Mr Canning. It did not even seem to occur to him that I might want to meet Mr Canning's companion. There was this same incomprehensible inability to see what I saw. All he wanted was to get out, but he wanted it very badly. He said,

'Hullo, Mac,' and I said, 'Hullo there, David,' and we smiled at each other like long lost brothers.

Mr Canning was looking at me now. He was looking at me in a sharp, penetrant sort of way, as if the very fact that he did not know anything about me was an attraction to him. David said, 'You don't know Mr Canning. This is Ian Mackellar.'

Mr Canning and I acknowledged each other. I looked at his companion, and she looked at me, but he did not introduce us. I do not think he was introducing her to anyone. He did not seem to have any manners at all. She had something plain and dark on, and next to no make-up. It all looked to me as faultless in its way as what she had been wearing in the train. I know very little about women's clothes, but I was sure hers were expensive. We looked at each other quite deliberately, as if there was no one else in the room. So far as I was concerned, there was not, in fact. Then we both smiled and nodded, very slightly, like two friends who meet at a stranger's party and exchange private signals. Mr Canning had asked if I was a writer too.

I took my eyes from hers just when she was starting to look amused again. I said, 'In a way, yes.' In fact my first book had had just enough life in it to allow them to take my second, and my second was barely afloat.

Mr Canning said, 'Mackellar? I don't think I know the name. Should I?'

I said, 'The cadet branch. The head of the family calls himself Strathairn. He makes biscuits.'

This pleased him, not because I had said it, but because he knew where he was now. He nodded. 'I know,' he said. 'And you write books?'

'Of a sort.'

David said, 'They're not bad, in fact. But he's young yet. I must be going, I'm afraid.' He nodded to Mr Canning and patted me lightly on the shoulder. He was barely a year older than I was, but he had written six or more, including a couple of sellers. He moved off towards the door, but was not half way there when he got into conversation with someone else I did not know. I did not know most of them.

Mr Canning said, 'What sort?'

'Novels.'

He nodded again. He nodded each time he added a fact to his collection. He said, 'Not as much money in them as in biscuits?'

She said, 'They're very good biscuits.' No wonder I had not heard her speak before. I could only just hear her now. The Cordelia syndrome.

I said, 'They are, aren't they? Are you a serious eater?'

'I like the Jubilee Creams.'

I nodded gravely. I could nod as well as the next man. 'Ah,' I said, 'the sixty-eight ones. A hundred years of British biscuit making. But not one of the best years, in fact. I'm a wafers man myself. Lemon Fingers, now.'

'I know,' she said. 'A nice bouquet, but a bit light for me. There's a good coffee one. I forget—'

'That would be the Mocha Slips,' I said. 'I'm against a coffee flavour myself. I mean, except in coffee.'

Mr Canning was looking from one to the other of us. I do not think he moved his head at all, only his eyes. He was not a man to commit himself more than he need. He looked faintly puzzled and resentful. I thought he was not resentful, as the ordinary man might have been, because he was being left out, but resentful because he was puzzled. There was something here he did not know, and he could not bear that. It was not the biscuits he minded about. Anyone knows about biscuits. He said, 'Do you two know each other?' There was no jealousy in it at all. It was only as if it had not occurred to him that she might know anyone.

12

I was not going to say a word. I just looked at her, and Mr Canning went on looking at both of us. She said, 'We have met, yes.'

The party had suddenly gone quiet, and when I took my eyes off her, I saw that people were drifting away fast and the room already half empty. Mr Canning saw it too. He turned and made for the door. She went after him, and I went with her. Right in the doorway he ran into Mr Charteris, Penelope's Alastair, and they started talking. I did not hear what either of them said. I said, 'Please can we meet some time?'

She looked at me a little doubtfully. 'If you like,' she said. She did not seem to understand either. 'I'll see if I can manage it. Can you give me a phone number?'

I gave it to her and she nodded. She did not write it down or anything, but I knew she would remember it, just as she had remembered seeing me in the train. Then Mr Canning said good-bye to Mr Charteris and went on out, and she went out after him. I was left facing Mr Charteris. For a moment he looked at me blankly, and then he put on his professional smile. 'Hullo,' he said. 'I'm sorry I haven't seen anything of you. Been such a crowd. Always the way at these parties.' We talked amicably for a few minutes. I still did not know at the end of it whether he knew who I was, but he knew enough to find out. He probably asked Penelope later. I said my good-byes and went.

I walked northwards through Bloomsbury, going slowly. It was a still night, slightly foggy but not really cold. I had had enough to drink to set my mind working, but not enough to confuse the issues. I knew pretty well what had happened to me, and I was weighed down with an enormous mixture of apprehensions. I was terribly afraid I might not hear from her, and I knew that if I did not, there would be nothing I could do about it. In another part of my mind I was terribly afraid of what might happen

13

if I did. There was something completely new here, and I could not cope with it at all.

Nevertheless, for the next ten days or so I behaved very sensibly. In all physical respects I lived my normal life, which meant that I went out soon after breakfast, leaving no one to answer the phone if it did ring. After all, you did not expect to find people at home during the day. You might try, but if there was no reply, you tried again in the evening. If the thing was urgent enough, you might even try in the early morning, but I did not for a moment suppose that for her there was any sort of urgency in it. In the evenings I gave up all pretence of being sensible, and simply sat over the phone. If anyone asked me, I said I was working. I was not, in fact, but then I should not have been in any case, not really working. I was in between books, and I should really have been brooding over the next. As it was, there was only one thing I brooded about. It was only my physical life that was in any way normal.

Various people did ring up, of course, but the moment I picked up the receiver, I knew where I was with them, even if it was a woman speaking. I did not know anyone else with a voice even remotely like hers. Jimmy rang up once, in a fairly buoyant mood. Jimmy was my agent, and a friend of mine. He was not one of the big ones, but I thought he was good. After all, he had sold a couple of beginner's books, and to a respectable publisher. That was good enough for me. We had not reached the point yet where he had to haggle with M.G.M. over the film-rights. He told me that there had been a couple of good late notices, and the book was starting to move. He wanted to know what I was doing about the next. The thing was to have a quick follow-up ready in case this one really took. I put him off as best I could.

It must have been just about ten days after the party that the phone went quite late at night. It was a man's voice, with some sort of local accent I could not place. He said

14

would I accept a call from Studham. I said I would. There was the usual click, and then she said, 'Mr Mackellar?' Her voice came very clearly over the line. For all its smallness, it was the sort of voice that did.

I said, 'Speaking. Hullo.'

She said, 'Hullo. I'm sorry to make you pay for the call. I'm in a call-box, and I found I hadn't got the coins. I didn't want not to ring at all.'

I was very calm and friendly. 'I'm very glad you did,' I said. 'Do you mind telling me your name? No one's told me yet.'

'Oh – Julia.'

'Julia what?'

She hesitated. Then she said, 'Mellors.'

'Really?'

'Yes. Why?'

'I thought you hesitated.'

'I wasn't making it up. Only I wasn't sure it was any use telling you.'

I said, 'Mellors, like the gamekeeper?'

'That's right. No relation.'

'I'm glad of that. Not one of my favourite characters.'

There was quite a pause. Then she said, 'Look, I'm afraid we can't meet. I had to leave London, and I couldn't ring you before. Only I didn't want not to ring when you'd asked me to.'

'When will you be back, then?'

'I don't know. Some time, perhaps.'

'Will you ring me then?'

She hesitated again. Then she said, 'I'll try. But I don't know when it will be.'

I said, 'Please do.' There was nothing more I could say.

She said again, 'I'll try. I must ring off now, or it will cost you the earth. Good-bye, Mr Mackellar.'

'The name is Ian. My friends call me Mac.'

'I know. Good-bye, then, Ian.'

15

I said, 'Good-bye, Julia,' and she rang off.

I put the receiver down. Then I lifted it again and dialled enquiries. They came on the line quite quickly, and it was a man again. They are always quicker and more helpful at night. I think they get bored. I said, 'Can you tell me where the Studham exchange is?'

CHAPTER TWO

When I came to Rainsburgh, I stopped and went into a call-box. The local directory had been savaged, and the list of places covered was missing, but I went straight for the M.s, and even on my way there a couple of Studham numbers caught my eye. Directory Enquiries had not let me down. There were quite a lot of Mellorses. I did not know whether it was a local name, or whether I should have found an equal number in other local directories. Three of them were on the Studham exchange. One was a newsagent in High Street. One was J. Mellors, who lived at Windbarrow Farm, East Clanstead. One was Lt Col. H. M. F. Mellors, who lived at The Grange, Uppishley. There was also, no doubt, a gamekeeper somewhere, but his cottage would not be on the phone.

I ignored the newsagent. Remembering Julia's clothes, I thought the colonel more likely than the farmer, but you could never tell these days. For all he lived at Uppishley Grange, H.M.F. might be a lean chap eking out a part-commuted pension by repairing furniture and doing up-holstery jobs, whereas J. might have hundreds of acres of prime arable and drive round in a Bentley. And of course I had to face the considerable possibility that neither of them was anything to do with Julia. She might have been fifty miles from home when she telephoned. She might not be on the phone at all, and indeed the fact that she had used a call-box would suggest to any but the irrational mind that she was not. Mercifully, so far as Julia was concerned, I did not lack irrationality. I took H.M.F. to win and J. for a place.

While I was about it, I turned back to the C.s on the chance of finding a Canning. This was a long shot, because I had placed Mr Canning as a city type if ever there was one, but I came up straight away with a surprisingly strong runner. There was a Canning & Barfield, Solicitors, also in Studham High Street, perhaps handy to the news-agent's. I had suspected Mr Canning of law as soon as I heard him talking to David, though I had got the branch wrong. I now saw him as a senior partner of the family solicitors, who had come up to town, unwillingly, with Julia on family business. He was an old acquaintance of Mr Charteris, and had button-holed him at the Athenaeum or somewhere. Mr Charteris, faced with this grim visitant from the country and the appalling prospect of having to give it lunch, had fobbed him off with the office party. I did not like to think that a family solicitor could treat the daughter of one of his old clients the way Mr Canning appeared to treat Julia, but perhaps he treated everyone like that. Indeed, from what I had seen of him I thought he very probably did. Anyhow, so far as I was concerned, Mr Canning was only a handy cross-reference and as such I had great hopes of him. I got back into the car and drove on into Studham. There was no Mellors Arms, but the King's Head gave me a room only two doors from the bathroom. I put my case upstairs and went out to buy the local Ordnance Survey sheet.

East Clanstead was west of Studham, though naturally

not as far west as West Clanstead. Uppishley was a bit east of north. They both looked small on the map, but they had probably grown since. Both the Grange and Wind-barrow Farm were marked. Neither was more than three or four miles out. I unpacked and drank an early cup of tea. Then I got the car out again and drove northwards.

It was pretty country, with enough up and down in it to avoid monotony, but rich enough to spread on bread and butter. As I had expected, Uppishley had grown a bit since the last survey, but I saw at once that I need not have worried about the colonel's pension. The Grange was not a big house, but it had everything for its size, including what looked like stables in use. The house itself was old stone lovingly looked after, and every bit of woodwork in sight had been painted the day before yesterday. There were no farm buildings, only gardens and the usual offices. If the colonel farmed, he farmed elsewhere. The land round might have been anybody's. From what I had now seen of him, I did not place him with a Rolls, unless it was a veteran. I thought he probably drove a Rover with a towing bracket for the horse-box, or perhaps something smaller, with a Landrover for the horses.

I did not go in. I am no good at pretending to be an insurance salesman, and if this was where Julia lived, I did not want to upset her. Besides, I had all the time in the world. In view of what followed, I want to make this clear. I may have been acting a bit oddly, but according to my lights I was immensely serious. I had come here the morning after Julia had telephoned, but I should have done the same if she had telephoned from Brisbane. It was not im-petuosity so much as a simple inability to do anything else. All the same, I still did not know if this was where she lived, though it fitted the picture. I stopped the car outside long enough to take it all in. Then I drove back and parked in a field-gate just outside the village. According to the survey there were a couple of pubs, but they would not be open now. Everybody knows that if you want local knowledge, you go to the pub. If you are prepared to make direct enquiries, the post office is better, but I was not. For slanted conversation the pub is the place, because that is where the conversation occurs. This may have come as a revelation to a town-type like Dr Watson, but any countryman has known it for the last five centuries at least. In the meantime, I parked here between the Grange and the village. I might see the colonel go driving by. Or even Julia herself. I did not really expect this, but anything could happen. In any case I was content to wait. I had all the rest of my life for what I had in mind.

In point of fact, I did see the colonel, though only for a moment. The car came very quietly from behind, and was alongside me almost before I was ready for it. He turned and looked at me, of course. Anyone would in a place like that. It was only a glance as his car went by, but I could have sworn to the family face. I suppose it was the eyes in fact, but mainly it was the expression and the way he looked at me. It was a serious, considering face, absolutely assured but free of all assertion. But above all, it was the way he drove. There are few things more absolutely characteristic of a man nowadays than the way he drives, and in a country lane you see it as under a magnifying glass. That was why I had not heard him until he was almost on me, he went with such quiet competence. I had not seen Julia drive, but I knew she would drive just like that. I did not even notice the car, but it was certainly nothing very noticeable.

Once I had been seen there, I did not want to stay, so I backed out and drove through the village to the other side. I could see only one pub, but the other might have lost its licence and shut down. Even this one was not the Mellors Arms. It was the Morning Star, which was nice and new to me. I went in there later, and they told me, in the course of conversation, that the colonel had no children.

This was a set-back, but no more. I had seen the colonel, and knew I was not far wrong. There were lots of other possibilities. Julia might even be a very much younger sister. There was certainly some relationship. It is easy enough to imagine a merely physical likeness, but not that look on a face. Of course, Julia might not live here at all. She might have been merely staying with relations. I thought that would explain her reluctance to put through a long-distance call on the house telephone. But at least I was at one end of a clear line, and it would lead me to her sooner or later. Meanwhile there was Windbarrow Farm to be looked at. Families still lived in neighbourhoods, at least in this sort of country. I drove out to East Clanstead next morning.

The farm was a real farm, all right, still very much in working order. There was a long, low brick house, pleasant enough, with gardens in front of it, but behind it there was the usual gaggle of modern farm buildings, no doubt highly efficient but dreadful to look at. Considering that they had some of the most beautiful sites in the world to build on, I could never see why the designers of farm buildings should not be given at least some rudimentary training in aesthetics, but all too clearly they were not, and the farmers themselves were the last people to care. The site here was particularly pleasant. The farm was on the slope of a hill with a shallow valley in front. Down in the valley a good-sized brook wandered through its willows, and above the buildings the hill ran up in a soft curve topped with the green tumulus it no doubt took its name from. Even fifty years ago, with the sort of buildings they had then, it would have been as pretty as a picture. Now it would be a very nice place to live, but no one would want to paint it. Still, it was prosperous enough. J. Mellors might no longer wear breeches and gaiters, but he could afford to dress Julia, if he did dress her, the way she was. I drove a few hundred yards past the gate and parked in the lane, close in to the hedge.

20

I thought I would leave the car and walk round a bit, and you cannot leave a car in a field-gate in case someone wants to get in or out. Anything short of a combine-harvester could get past it where it was, and it was not the time of the year for those.

I went on down the lane the way I had been going, heading down into the valley. I did not know how the farm lands lay, but a brook of this size nearly always has a field-path running along it one side or the other, and it would be a pleasant place to walk on a morning like this. As far as I could see, the valley was all pasture. If the farmer had any arable, it would be higher up, but whether or not he crossed the brook, he plainly had a good deal of money in milk and stock. I found the path on the other side of the road bridge, and set out along it. It may have been five minutes later that I got over a stile in a quickset hedge and almost fell over a young man sitting on the bank. There ought to be fishing in a stream of that size, but he was not fishing. He was not doing anything. He was just sitting there looking down at the water.

He was a very fair young man, really startlingly fair. Despite the fact that I had almost fallen over him, he did no more than turn his head and look up at me. His eyes were very large and blue and his features very delicate. It was the sort of face that made you feel at once, if you were a man of normal propensities, that he ought to have been a woman. It had no expression in it at all. He stared at me like that for what seemed quite a long time, but was probably in fact no more than a second. Then he turned back to the water again. After a bit he smiled, but he must have been smiling to himself, because all he was looking at was the water. Then he turned his face up to me again and included me in the smile. It was a sweet smile on that face, but a little remote, as if he was not quite in focus. He said, 'Where are you off to? You'll only get to Grainger's that way. Is that where you're going?' His voice was the ordinary voice of an educated young man. There was nothing rustic about him.

I smiled back at him. The tone of his question had been a little pettish, and I had a strong, immediate instinct to keep on the right side of him. I did that, in fact, literally, because I sat down on the bank beside him, still smiling pleasantly. 'I don't know where I'm going,' I said. 'Just for a walk. I saw the path and came along it. I hope I'm not trespassing.'

He had turned his face back to the water when I sat down beside him, and now all he gave me was a quick sideways flicker of the eyes. 'Oh no,' he said. 'There's a right of way, in fact, but not many people use it.'

He did not ask me any further questions. To me, with my private question big in my mind, it seemed that for me to be merely going for a walk, at that time and place, called loudly for some explanation, but he did not seem to see it like that. So long as I was not going to Grainger's, he had no further interest. I almost wished he had asked me. At least it would have kept the conversation going. As it was, I sat there beside him, also staring at the water and wondering what to say.

Then he whipped out a hand and grabbed me by the arm. It was so sudden that I felt I had jumped inches clear of the bank, but his grip on my arm was extremely strong. I turned and looked at him. My mouth must have been a little open. His face was ablaze with pleasure and excitement, and he was pointing at something with his free hand. It all happened so quickly that when my eyes followed his hand, I still had time to get a glimpse of some small sleek body on the farther edge of the water. It was gone even as I looked at it. There was a ripple on the water below it, but I could not tell whether it had gone out of the water into the bank or off the bank into the water. He said, 'Did you see him?' He spoke in an eager whisper.

I nodded. I wished he would let go of my arm. 'Just,' I said. 'What was he?'

'Water rat,' he said. His fingers gradually relaxed their grip. 'They've got a nest in there. That was the male. I haven't seen the young yet. They'll be out soon. That's really something.'

I asked the first question that came into my head. He had dropped his hand now, and I really wanted to know. 'How do you know it was a male?' I said.

He looked at me with interest. He seemed politely puzzled. 'Know?' he said. 'Well, I know him by sight. I mean, they're quite different. Different shape. Different way of moving.' He seemed almost apologetic now, as if he realised he was being unreasonable. 'I see a lot of them, of course,' he said. He seemed suddenly aware of his oddity and anxious to minimise it, so that I in turn became slightly ashamed of the way I had felt when he grabbed at me like that.

I said, 'Of course. You're very lucky.' I had not meant to leave it at that. What I had been going to say was that he was very lucky to have the time to watch his furry friends like this, but I saw as soon as I had started to speak that I could not say this, because it implied an enquiry. It was on the face of it odd that a man of his age and apparent education should have nothing better to do than sit on the bank and watch water rats, but it would be an intrusion even to suggest this, and above all I did not want to intrude. So I left the sentence where it was, and even like that it sounded funny. I found him extraordinarily hard to talk to altogether.

He turned and looked at me, a full look this time, not just a flicker. 'You think I'm lucky?' he said. He said it in a serious, slightly puzzled way. Then his eyes flicked away from me sideways, and he smiled at the water. 'Perhaps I am,' he said.

After that neither of us said anything for quite a time. What I wanted above all was to get up and leave him, but

23

even this I found difficult. If I walked on along the path, I should only be going to Grainger's, whatever that was, and he knew I had nothing to take me there. If I walked back to the road, it would be even more pointed. So for a time I just sat there, and I was afraid all the time that one of the water rats would come out and he would grab my arm again.

I heard absolutely nothing until there was a gentle rustle in the grass on the other side of me and a voice said, 'Hullo.' I did not jump this time. It was not a voice to make you jump, at least not away from it. I turned quite deliberately and then caught my breath. It was the female counterpart, the one I had momentarily imagined when I had first found him sitting there, only my imagination had not done her justice. Apart from her looks, it was the way she looked at you. There was nothing secretive about her. Like Cressida, there was language in her eyes, her cheeks, her looks, and like Ulysses I set her down instantaneously as a daughter of the game.

'Hullo,' I said.

CHAPTER THREE

She said, 'What are you doing here?' She said it exactly as you say it to an old friend you meet unexpectedly in a strange place. She was as immediately familiar as he was remote.

I said, 'Nothing, really. I just came for a walk, and met your brother.' It never occurred to me to call him anything

24

else. The relationship was almost ludicrously obvious. In any case I did not know what else to call him. But when I had said it, I had a feeling that the thing needed clearing up a bit, and I said, 'Are you twins?'

'Not quite, but as near as nature permits without actually being. He's only just over a year younger. I think he was a mistake on someone's part. Probably Daddy's from what I know of Mummy.' She spoke almost as if he was not there, as in a sense I do not think he was. He was staring at the water again. He had looked round quickly when she arrived, but now he was taking no notice of either of us.

I said, 'It's a fantastic likeness.'

She nodded. 'He is pretty, isn't he?' she said. 'When we were younger, we used to dress alike sometimes for fun, and no one could tell the difference. We can't quite do it now.'

They could not, indeed, and did not. She was wearing something very skimpy and summery, with no shape of its own, the way they wear them now. Not that it needed any, with her inside it. It left very little to the imagination, and my imagination was very active. She went on looking at me. I was afraid that, unlike her brother, she was not going to be content with my explanation, and she was not. She said, 'What are you doing in these parts, then? We don't see many people. You're not a local, are you?'

I said, 'No, no. I was passing through, and stayed a night at the pub in Studham. Then this morning I came out this way, and saw the path and just came along it.' I did not think this would satisfy her either, so I went on to the attack. I said, 'Do you live at the farm?'

'That's right. There's nowhere else round here. Are you going on?'

'I don't know.' I looked at the water and then back at her again. 'I needn't, in fact, for a bit.'

I was almost angry with her for getting such an easy rise out of me, but with her it seemed impossible to help it. I knew that, like Cressida, she would make a coasting welcome ere it came, and sure enough she made it. She said, 'Don't go on yet. We need fresh faces.'

I said, 'I'll think about it.' I was back on the defensive now, and needed to be, but she smiled at me as if we had reached a complete understanding.

'Oh, good,' she said.

I had an urge to assure her that nothing had been decided, but that was nonsense. I could go away any time I wanted. It was just that I was still angry with her for hooking me so easily, as if I had been made a fool of by a child. I wondered how old they were, in fact, the pair of them. That sort of colouring makes any woman look very young until she is thirtyish, then the disaster can be absolute. But of course she was nowhere near that yet. She could not be. Meanwhile the conversation languished, but at least she had stopped asking questions.

I turned and looked at the brother. He was still staring at the water. I supposed he was waiting for the water rat, but his face was quite expressionless. I stared at the water myself, but I could see out of the corner of my eye that she was still looking at me. The trouble was that almost the only way you can talk to a woman like that is at very close range indeed, but I could not turn and grab her with her brother sitting there next to me, especially when I was still afraid that at any moment he might turn and grab me. We just sat there, the three of us, in the soft sunlight, and nothing made a sound, not even the water rats. It was a very odd situation altogether.

Then a voice called, 'Charlie! Beth! Where are you?' It came from the far side of the brook, and I knew it at once, but I could not see her. The willows grew thick there, hanging over the water, and she must have come down to it from the other side of them. We all three lifted our heads and looked towards the voice, but still she did not appear.

Then the boy, Charlie apparently, called out, 'Jule!

26

Jule, I'm here,' and I turned and looked at him because of the way he said it. His face was alight, not quite with excitement, but with a sort of radiant expectation. I looked at the far bank again. I could see her moving behind the trees, but she had not come out yet. Charlie sat motionless, following her with his eyes, and I turned and looked at the girl. There was no expectation here, only watchfulness. The eyes were slightly narrowed, and the mouth, which I had seen only smiling, was set close, so that you saw the faint beginnings of hardness at the corners. She saw me looking at her, and for a moment we looked at each other with a curious, muted calculation. Then the willow fronds parted and Julia came out on to the far bank, not more than four yards from us.

She stopped on the instant, and her eyes went to all our three faces in turn and then came back to mine. Then she smiled very slightly, but the concern did not go out of her face. She said, 'Hullo,' and her voice was the same as ever, very small and very clear.

She must have been wondering what to say, but there was no obvious indecision. She let her smile tide over the silence until Charlie broke it, as I suppose she knew he would. He got up suddenly and all in one movement. Then he took a couple of steps back and went forward again and cleared the brook at a bound. It was not Olympic stuff, but for a man who had been sitting there God knows how long before I got there, and had not moved more than his head and arms since, it was quite a performance. I remembered his grip on my arm, too. Now that he was on his feet, I could see that he was a good head shorter than I was, and he still had this curiously delicate appearance, but physically he was very formidable. He went up to Julia and put an arm round her waist, smiling at her. They were very much of a height. She turned her head and smiled at him. The two faces could hardly have been less alike, but in some way they were complementary, like the faces of

27

the Madonna and Child in the early pictures.

He said, 'Jule, I've seen the old man, but the young aren't out yet. I think they might have been, only this chap came along, and then Beth, and we were talking.' He smiled across the water at me, the ordinary social smile of a well-bred young man. 'I'm sorry,' he said, 'I don't know your name.'

Julia looked at me for just a moment. I was on my feet now. Then she turned back to him. She was still smiling, very slightly. 'Mr Mackellar,' she said.

His eyes flicked round to me and then back to Julia again. There was no expression in them at all, but he spoke in the correct tone of mild surprise. He said, 'Good lord, do you two know each other?'

She said, 'We've met once.' She was looking at me now. 'I didn't expect to see you here,' she said.

I said, 'Nor I you.' It was true as far as it went. And I still did not know what she was doing here or where they all fitted in.

She said, 'This is my brother Charlie. And that's my sister Beth.'

I had forgotten the girl was there, and when I turned round, I found that she was still sitting on the bank at my feet. It is difficult to bow to anyone who is sitting at your feet, but I made the most appropriate movement I could, and she smiled up at me. It was a slightly mocking smile, and behind the big blue eyes there was still a good deal of calculation. She kept her face turned up to me, but her eyes went sideways to Julia. 'We've met,' she said. 'Mr Mackellar is staying at the King's Head. He was just passing through but thinks he may stay on for a bit. That's if his other preoccupations permit.'

Julia said, 'Mr Mackellar is not as other men. He writes. I expect he can do his work anywhere. Or can't you?' It was all very pleasant and lightly handled.

I said, 'When I'm really working on a book, yes, pretty

well. I'm rather between books at the moment.'

Beth came in again, still from the grass at my feet. 'Well, that's fine,' she said. 'You can stay on either way. If you're looking for raw material, we've got plenty of that. And we need company, don't we, Jule?'

Julia said, 'I'm sure Mr Mackellar will please himself. I hope so, anyhow. Come on, Charlie. I want you up at the house.' The boy had taken his arm from her waist, and just for a moment he turned away from her and looked back at the stream. He did not say anything, and she did not say anything more. She just stood there, looking at him with an absolute concentration, as if they were the only two people in the world. The social smile had gone from her face. I cannot say what it was that had replaced it. I only know that if she had ever looked at me like that, I should have wanted nothing more, in this world or the next, but it was not me she was looking at. The silence probably lasted only a few seconds by the clock, but it felt as if time itself was being stretched to breaking point. I heard the faintest rustle beside me, and I knew that the girl had got up off the grass, but I did not turn round. Then Charlie smiled, to himself or at the water, I couldn't tell which, and turned the smile round to include Julia, exactly as he had done with me earlier. It seemed a long time ago now.

'Coming,' he said, and went up and slipped an arm through hers, and the two of them went off behind the willows.

Beth said, 'I'm not jumping over the brook myself, but don't let me stop you.'

I turned round to her, and we smiled cheerfully at each other. The world seemed a very easy place with only her and me in it. 'Not at the moment,' I said. 'I'm not sure I could, to tell the truth. With a run, I suppose. Not standing like that.'

She shook her head. 'Athletic type, Charlie. And yet he

29

hardly ever takes any exercise. There's a footbridge further down. Or we can walk back to the road.'

I said, 'Better the road, I think. I can't leave my car there indefinitely.'

'Ah, yes. I'd forgotten the car.' She hesitated as if she was going to say something, but thought better of it. 'Come on,' she said, 'let's go, then,' and we started walking back the way I had come. She was the same height as the other two. Like her brother, she had this uneasy combination of delicate features and colouring and an almost catlike physical efficiency, so that every movement seemed to flow from hidden reserves of energy. I was back with Cressida again, Cressida walking in a flowery summer slip of a dress beside an English brook, with her wanton spirits looking out at every joint and motive of her body.

I suppose Shakespeare had seen something of the sort walking by Avon in his impressionable years. I said, 'There's just the three of you?'

'That's right. Daddy died a couple of years ago.'

'And your mother?'

'She left us rather suddenly, I gather – oh, years back, when I was quite small. I don't think anyone knows where she's got to. She was like me and Charlie, to look at, I mean. I can just remember her. I thought she was marvellous. Jule's like Daddy.'

'Then who runs the farm?'

'Oh – Jule. She's one of the competent ones, Jule. You must have noticed?' So J. Mellors the farmer had been her all the time. It was just the sort of obvious probability you rejected as too simple.

I said, 'Well, I've only met her once, and that was at a publisher's party.' I wanted the fact established, and that, after all, was what the girl had wanted to know. 'No one looks very competent at a publisher's party. The only qualification needed is a loud voice, and she hasn't even got that. Oh, and she was with a chap who tended to hog the conversation anyway. A rather overpowering person called Canning.'

She laughed. Like everything else she did, the laugh bubbled up out of a sort of sheer physical exuberance. I thought she would have been marvellous on the stage, but she was out of her period. She belonged to the time of musical comedy, when people went to the theatre for the fun of it. And I reckoned she was hard enough, even for that. She said, 'Old George. What on earth was he doing there?'

'Search me. I think he knew one of the bosses and got himself asked. He didn't seem to be in his element exactly, but he was eager to learn.'

'He always is. And remembers it all, too. Did he cross-examine you?'

'Pretty well.'

'Then you're on the files. You may not know much about us, but believe me, we know all about you. Or can for the asking.'

I said, 'You're welcome to any extent you're interested. My life is an open book, and it wouldn't sell five hundred hardback. But who is this George Canning? I placed him as the family solicitor.' I did not think it necessary to mention my researches in the telephone directory.

'Well, that's what he is. Of course he had to do a lot when Daddy died suddenly like that, and then he sort of assumed he was going to take over the running of things. I mean, the farm and so on. From Jule, I mean. Well, I ask you. He's still struggling manfully, but of course he hasn't a hope.'

I said, 'I see, yes.' The colonel was obviously an uncle, the father's brother. I could not ask about him, but there was no real doubt. The father would have been just such a man, and he had married something very like Beth, an earlier model but the same make, and probably in a more inhibited age proportionately more lethal. The marriage

31

must in fact have lasted quite a while, but at what cost to the parties I did not like to think. Then the inevitable had happened, and Julia, at whatever age, had taken over the home just as she had now taken over the farm.

And Charlie, by the look of it. That was the remaining thing I had to know, and I not only could not ask it, I did not want to know it, except that of course I had to. All this time Beth was padding along beside me with the effortless grace of a cat taking a mouse for a walk in open country. Or perhaps not quite. It probably would not occur to the cat that the mouse might have alternative plans, and I thought Beth had her doubts already. She would not be one of the world's great intelligences, but in a matter like this her instincts would be deadly. We walked on in a silence full of unasked questions.

We were still some way from the road when we came to a stile, a high one, but with proper stepping boards. All the fencing was good. I stood back to let her negotiate it, which she did with some very uninhibited leg-work. When she was over, she turned suddenly and leant on it with her arms spread and her breasts buoyed up maddeningly on the top rail. I had already come up to climb it myself, but now I fetched up short, and we stood there facing each other, very close, but with the stile separating our working parts, like a pair of friendly livestock conversing over the fence between their fields. I put my hands on the rail too, but spread wide on each side of her. Just for a moment her eyes went down to my hands, first one then the other. Then she looked at me again and smiled. She said, 'I do like you. What's your name?'

'Ian,' I said, 'but most people just say Mac.'

She ran a considering eye over me and nodded. 'Mac's all right,' she said. 'You don't wear a kilt or anything, do you?'

I said, 'Och, awa, not since I was a wee bairn.' I gave it the full Harry Lauder treatment.

She said, 'What's the good of a kilt on a wee bairn?'

I returned to English. 'Anyway,' I said, 'I don't.'

She nodded, but regretfully. She said, 'What does Jule call you?'

'She calls me Mr Mackellar.'

She gave a sort of small snort, but offered no comment. Instead she said, 'What sort of books do you write?'

'I have in fact written two, both different. Well, I mean, both novels, but different. I expect the next will be different, too. My genius is burgeoning.'

'Good for it. Can you live on it?'

'Not yet. Better soon, I hope. I don't have to, in fact.'

'You mean you've got money of your own?'

I sighed. 'You can ask Old George,' I said. 'He'll tell you all about it. But yes. My family makes biscuits. They have been making biscuits since 1868. You can't make biscuits on that scale without making a certain amount of money on the side, and some of it has brushed off on me. I'm not what you'd call gilded, but I needn't starve if I'm careful.'

'But you don't actually take a hand at the biscuit-making yourself?'

'Not personally. Nor at the baby foods, nor at the breakfast foods, nor even at the pet foods. No doubt I could have, and it would have been well regarded. But I was meant for higher things.'

'But the money helps?'

'It helps like hell. Very few people really write well until they've stopped worrying about the rent.'

She had been sinking slowly on her arms, until the rail was practically pushing her breasts out of the top of her dress. I looked down at them. I did not know what I was going to do about them or her, not feeling as I did about Julia, and her her sister. I said, 'I think you had better let me get over the stile. I can't with you like that, not without stepping on something.'

She straightened up slowly, and I watched them slip back

33

into their proper receptacles. Then she stood back. 'Come on,' she said. 'I'm not stopping you.'

I got over and started walking straight ahead. She hesitated a moment and then fell into step beside me. We did actually walk in step, for all the difference in height. When we came to the road, she looked up at my car, still nestling under the hedge. She said, 'That your car?'

'That's it.'

She said, 'Good old biscuits. Will you give me a lift to the house?'

I was already resigned to this. 'I suppose so,' I said.

CHAPTER FOUR

I remember when I was a child falling in love with the elder sister of a friend of mine. He was a good friend of my own age, and at one time, I think when I was about twelve, I used to see a lot of him during the school holidays. We went to different schools, but lived near enough, given bicycles, to be in and out of each other's houses most of the time when we were at home. That was for as long as the intense friendship lasted, which was probably not very long in fact. People grow up different, and the differences soon show. But while it lasted, his sister was my lodestar. I cannot remember much what she looked like, but I remember she had a queenly quality and beautiful breasts. I suppose she was seventeen or thereabouts. All this talk of calf love and wanting to be mothered is nonsense. A boy falls in love with an older woman because only an older woman is in herself sexually interesting. (At the other end of life it works the other way, of course.) I did not want Daphne – I think she was Daphne, and it was still just the Daphne period – I did not want Daphne to mother me, I wanted to make love to her, though at that stage I had only the vaguest idea how to set about it. I remember I always hoped she would let herself get involved in our physical brawling, so that I could get hold of her and perhaps feel her breasts, but she never would. She was too queenly for that. She knew of my passion, of course, and played up to it in the nicest kind of way. That also is a commonplace. A young woman responds to passion even in a much younger boy, though she has to be very short of older company to do anything about it physically. Then you do get the queer cases. But Daphne did not lack company, and all she had for me was a sort of playful tenderness. I shared it, unwillingly, with her brother, and gave her in return my total devotion.

The situation at Windbarrow was not really the same, but it had a touch of the same desperation. After all, I was older than Julia, though not much. At any rate, I was of an age for her, and I was quite a lot older than Charlie and Beth. Not that this worried Beth, or indeed at first even Charlie. But Julia felt herself of a different generation from them, and relegated me, from the start, to their generation, not hers. Not quite to their generation, because she did not feel in any way responsible for me. On the contrary, she assumed that I must share her sense of responsibility for the others. It was more as if I was an older child in a group of children, so that I was subject to the same disabilities, but more was expected of me. I suppose it was the way she had been regarded herself when she was a child, at least by her father. I resented her attitude bitterly, but found it extraordinarily hard to break down. I did break it down finally, and when I did the consequences were disastrous.

It was Beth who made the running, of course. I would not go her pace, but at least she gave me some sort of ostensible reason for staying on. Julia did me the curious, double-edged justice of knowing it was not my real reason, but it enabled her, too, to accept a situation she might not otherwise have tolerated. I saw very little of her that first day or two. She always seemed to be busy, and when I did see her, I was always with the others, which meant that I could not, except in the sense of mere physical presence, be with her. She would not join us in anything we did. She knew I wanted to be with her, of course, and used the others as a defensive screen to make sure I was not. This apart, it really was uncannily like Daphne all over again.

At the end of the second day I decided to write to her. This may seem an odd thing to do, but the whole situation was odd. I find it in any case much easier to say what I mean on paper than by word of mouth, but the main thing was that I was convinced that there was something that needed saying. I knew I was not in myself repugnant to her. That after all is a thing which the great majority of people, men and women, really do know. Whatever the barrier was, it was one she deliberately interposed, and it was not only me that was to be held back by it. To some extent, to a lesser extent obviously, but still to some extent, it was herself too. I spent a good part of the night turning over in my head what I wanted to say, and in the morning after breakfast I sat down in the stiff deserted writing room of the King's Head to say it.

I had done no more than square myself up to the paper when the door opened and Beth came in. There was no hesitation about it, no putting her head round the door to see if I was there and if I was alone. She had obviously found all that out downstairs. She opened the door quietly and slipped in, shutting it behind her. I was sitting at a writing table with my back to the door, and had looked over my shoulder when the door opened. For a moment she stood with her back to the door, looking at me. She was wearing trousers, very close-fitting, with some sort of floppy top. She generally had worn trousers ever since the first time I saw her. So far as I was concerned, that was a mistake, but I was not going to tell her so. I was glad of all the extra defences I could get.

My immediate feeling was relief that I had not yet actually put pen to paper. I knew that if I had, she would have tried to see what I was writing, and I should have had to cover it up or turn it over to prevent her, and this would have involved us in explanations. It was for all the world like a man caught by a jealous wife writing a love letter to someone else. This was so ridiculous that it made me angry. Beth often did make me angry, or at least irritated me intensely. It was my main defence against her. I put my pen down on the still blank paper and turned round to face her. I turned as far as I could on the chair, and then picked the chair up and turned that round too. I made slightly heavy weather of the whole thing, because I wanted her to understand that I had been busy and she was disturbing me. It was true, of course, but all the time I was conscious of playing up to her, and that made me angrier than ever.

I do not think she was aware of my anger, or if she was, she took no notice of it. She ignored my anger, which was real but mainly for my own consumption, and went straight for my show of reluctance, which was put on, or at least exaggerated, but meant for her. She would take you on any terms provided it was her you were concerned with. Nothing else interested her. She said, 'Oh, Mac, I am sorry. Shall I go?'

'No,' I said. 'Where's Charlie?'

She left the door then and came slowly across the room and stood just in front of me. There were other chairs in the room, but they were the usual unsympathetic hotel chairs, and ranged round the wall. I could hardly blame her

37

for not going and sitting on any of them. I ought to have got up from where I was sitting, but I did not, because that was part of the act. So she came and stood there in front of me, with my face just below the point where the soft stuff flowed down over her breasts like water over a water-fall and just above the skin-tight crotch of those damned trousers. She said, 'Charlie?' in a small, remote voice, as if she did not want to break in on what she knew I was really thinking about.

'Yes,' I said, 'Charlie, your young brother. Don't you remember?' I got up out of my chair. This brought me that much closer to her, but at least I was looking down at her face and not straight across at the middle of her body, and that made her much easier to talk to. For all its prettiness, her face was not what you looked at naturally when you looked at her, or what you remembered when you thought of her. With Julia I never looked at anything else. I wanted all of her, but the whole of her was there in her face. I could have made love to Beth in a Guy Fawkes mask.

I moved back, pushing my chair back until I felt it come up against the writing table. We were still close, but out of kissing distance, and the great thing was that I had moved back, not forward.

She showed no sign of defeat, but her voice came out at a normal pitch. She said, 'Charlie's having one of his bad days.'

I walked away from her sideways and sat down on one of the other chairs against the wall. She sat down on the chair I had left. She may have got some satisfaction out of it, but I think not much. I said, 'Beth, tell me about Charlie. It's no business of mine, really, but after all I have seen quite a bit of him. I can't make him out. He's perfectly normal and pleasant one minute, young for his age but quite normal, and the next he's just not there. And you can't do anything about it, just wait for him to come back.'

She said, 'Well, he's hopped to the wide, of course. I mean, whenever you see him.'

'You mean drugged?'

'Well, yes. Sedated, anyway. I don't mean he's on it himself. He has to have it fed to him. Otherwise he couldn't go out.'

I suppose I had really known all along what I was up against, even from that first time on the river bank when I had seen him and Julia together. But I had put off facing it, and even now I did not know the full extent of it. But I had to, of course. There was no going back now. I said, 'But what's the trouble, Beth?'

She leant back in her chair with her legs stretched straight out in front of her, so that her whole body was almost in a straight line. Her hands were folded in her lap, and her face was tilted forward, staring at them. It was an entirely male pose. I suppose the trousers had something to do with it, but mainly it was that for the moment she had forgotten herself and was thinking about someone else. I had a sudden, disconcerting glimpse of a hard, masculine mind lurking in that aggressively feminine body. She said, 'Well, he's bonkers, poor Charlie. Not – not mental, exactly. I mean, he can think all right. He's clever actually. But emotionally. He gets over-excited, and then he can be violent. It's a family thing, I gather. I think Mummy had a brother no one ever saw.'

'Has he always been like this?'

'No. It's – well, fairly recent. I mean, he was at school and all that like anybody else, but then there were incidents, and they took him away just before he'd done his full time, and he's been at home ever since. When you say he's young for his age – well, I mean, of course he is, he hasn't had a chance to grow up really, not since then. And what you say about his coming and going, that's the dope, of course, That and – well, you see, he knows about himself. He's too intelligent not to. Sometimes he resents it and sometimes he takes advantage of it, but he knows about it all the time, even when he's hopped. You know when you're drunk? Because you're drunk you do odd things, but all the time you're there inside yourself, seeing yourself going on like that, and thinking how odd it all is. I reckon it's like that with him. His mind's clear, you see, under it all. I mean, he doesn't think he's Napoleon or anything. He knows he's Charlie Mellors, hopped, or acting queer, or both. It can't be nice.'

I sat there staring in front of me, just as she was. We neither of us looked at each other at all during the whole conversation, but I think we were more on terms with each other at that moment than we ever were before it or after. Finally I said, 'But can it go on? Won't they have to—?'

'Put him away? I suppose so, if he gets worse. Or if he gets into any real trouble. But you couldn't do it now, could you?'

I pushed the knife right home. I did not need to, but I took a sort of hopeless satisfaction in it. I said, 'But who looks after him, then?'

'Oh, Jule, of course. She can do anything with him, whatever state he's in. She's the only one who can. I mean, the doctor's in and out and all that, but Jule does it all. Not that there's much to do, physically, I mean. There's nothing wrong with him physically. It's a matter of managing him.'

I said, 'And loving him,' and her head snapped up and for the first time we looked at each other.

She gave a little wry smile. 'I suppose so,' she said. 'I wouldn't know. Poor Jule and poor Charlie.' Her face went down again, but I went on watching her. She said, 'When are you going?' She said it to her hands.

'I don't know,' I said, and she pulled her legs in and got slowly to her feet. She went to the door, and looked at me, once, very quickly, just before she got there.

'Don't go yet,' she said. 'Now you go on with whatever

you were doing. I'm sorry I disturbed you.' Then she opened the door and went out.

I went back and turned the chair round again to face the writing table and sat down on it, facing my blank paper. I sat there staring at the paper, but I did not write anything on it, because now I had nothing more to say. After a bit I gathered up my writing things and went up to my room and put them away. Then I went downstairs and out of the house and got my car out. I did not know where Beth was. She might be shopping in the town or might by now be on her way back to Windbarrow. In any case, I did not want to see her. I drove straight out of the town eastwards, away from Windbarrow, through country I had not seen before.

I do not suppose my state of mind was a very admirable one. In fact, I know it was not. I know, looking back, that the poison was already in my system and starting to work. Above all, I was full of an enormous sense of injustice, and that is dangerous stuff. If I had loved Julia in a less respectable sort of way, I might have found at least a mental way through the thicket, whatever came of it physically. But I loved her very much as a person, and I saw with a sort of despairing certainty that, being the person she was, she was bound to do what she was doing. There was no way out of the thing at all, but my mind went round and round inside it, battering at the walls of the trap, and getting sorer all the time.

What emerged was a determination to see her, to get her to myself and make her understand what she was doing to me. Writing was no good now. It was no longer explanations that were needed. I had all the explanations I wanted. Also, I knew the kind of letter she would write if I wrote to her, and I knew that once it was there, on paper, there would be no getting round it and nothing more I could do. The thing must not be allowed to go that far. I must get at her first and shatter her peace and assurance, and bring her

41

reason down to the level of my own unreasonableness, because that was my only hope if I was not going to give her up altogether. I suppose I must have known that this was selfish and unkind of me, but I dared not let myself see it like that. All I could see was that there was something here of incalculable value to me, and I told myself to her, and I was determined that it must be thrust on her until she too found it impossible to give up.

All the same, there was nothing I could do about it immediately. I did not know what one of Charlie's bad days involved, but I had to assume that they kept Julia fully occupied. Also, I had the sense to see, even in the state of mind I was in, that this was not the best time to try the sort of approach I had to make. If I was irrelevant to the general run of her life, I was doubly irrelevant at a time like this. I drove back to Studham somewhere around midday with the idea of packing and going back to London. It seemed the only thing I could possibly do, but I did not know whether, when it came to the point, I could do it.

CHAPTER FIVE

I did not go back to London, not then, nor did I write my letter. I spent the rest of the day unhappily doing nothing, and next morning I phoned Windbarrow and got Julia. I said, 'I want to speak to you. Can you find the time?'

There was a pause. Then she said, 'Wait a moment,' which I was already doing. When her voice came on again, it started a little remote and then came closer. I had not heard anything, but I had the feeling that she had gone away from the phone and then come back to it. She said, 'Can I ring you back? I'm very busy just at the moment.'

I said, 'I'm in a call-box at the pub.' I gave her the number. 'I'll wait about by the box till you ring. If someone else goes in, I can't stop them. So if you find the number engaged, try again. I'll still be here. But I don't think anyone will.'

She said, 'All right,' and put down the receiver.

The call-box was in the passage next to the bars. It was not the ideal place to wait, but at least no one was likely to see me waiting at this time of day. Not that there was any good reason why they should not, but I did not want them to. I think what really worried me was the possibility that Beth might find me there before Julia's call came, just as she had found me on the point of writing to her. In everything that had to do with Julia I had this curious sense of surveillance, and God knows things were difficult enough without that. I did not even quite believe that Julia had been busy – not too busy to talk to me even for a moment. I had the feeling that she did not want to talk to me just then, but preferred to pick her own time later, and if this was so, it must be because the wrong person, or at any rate someone, was with her. And she had been so abrupt and uncommunicative. Now that I came to think of it, she had not said a single word over the phone which would identify me to whoever was with her. It was all like something in a spy thriller. I did not see why all this secretiveness was necessary, and I resented it. Meanwhile I stood in the passage and waited for the phone in the box to ring. The passage was rather dark and smelt faintly of beer. I felt silly hanging about there, and I hated feeling silly over something I minded so desperately about.

I waited for a surprisingly long time, feeling unhappier with every minute that passed. At least no one came, and

I did my waiting in private. When the bell rang in the box, I went in at once and picked up the receiver while the door swung shut on its spring behind me. All I could hear was a series of pips. I gave my number, and then there was a click and the pips stopped, and Julia's voice came on the line. It was not until after she had rung off that I realised what all this meant.

Now I said again, 'Julia, I very much want to speak to you. Can we please meet somewhere where we can talk?'

This time there was no hesitation. After all, she knew what I was going to say and must have made up her mind what to say to it. And this time there was nothing to stop her saying anything. She said, 'Yes, all right. Look, have you seen the barrow up on the hill behind the farm?'

'Yes, I know.'

'Well, I often walk up there. I'll try to go up this afternoon, somewhere about three. Could you find your way up there, do you think? Only – only don't come by the farm, do you mind? I'll explain when we meet.'

I said, 'I'll be up there before three. And I'll come up from the far side – what do I mean? – yes, from the east. Will that be all right?'

'Oh yes, thank you. I'm sorry – Anyhow, see you then.'

She rang off and I still stood there, in the box, thinking. It was only then that it occurred to me that Julia had phoned me only twice, and that both times she had gone out of the house and used a call-box. This did not make me any happier.

However, I had got what I wanted. I was going to see her this afternoon, and in circumstances which would let me say what I had to say. It was relief I felt rather than anything like exhilaration. At least the desperate frustration of the last few days was over. Whatever it was I was up against, I was going to be able to get to grips with it. But I did not for a moment let myself see this as a lovers' meeting. On the contrary, I was full of apprehension of the

44

outcome and of my own total inability, even when we did meet, to influence it in any way. I suppose the man in the dock is relieved when he sees the jury coming back, but that was about all there was to it. I gave up trying to think what I was going to say to her. My head had been full of phrases for days now, but I knew that when it came to the point, I should not use any of them. They were for the letter I had never written. By way of doing something useful, I got out the Survey sheet and started to work out my route for coming up to the hill-top from the far side, so that I did not come within sight of the farm. I saw at once that it was not going to be easy, and would in any case involve a good deal of walking. But I had plenty of time, more time than I wanted or knew what to do with, and I was glad of a practical problem and of the exercise involved.

I had an early bread-and-cheese lunch, and was out of the pub by a quarter past one. After a bit I drove slowly, looking for a lane that turned off northwards a mile or so before East Clanstead. It was uncoloured on the map, and I was looking for something pretty small, but even so I missed it the first time. There was nothing to say it was there or where it went to. There was just a gap in the hedge and this thin ribbon of tarmac going off to the right between other hedges and away into the fields, pointing nowhere in particular. If I met anything bigger than a bicycle, one of us would have to back to the nearest gate, but I did not think I should at this time of day. The lunch-hour is as sacred in the country as it is in the city.

After a bit I stopped and went back to the map. I memorised the general run of the lane to make sure I was in the right one. Then I tried to fix the point where I must leave the car and start walking. I reckoned that after about half a mile the ground would start to rise fairly steeply on my left and the lane would jink that way in a sharp elbow, probably following a contour. If I could find anywhere to put it, the point of the elbow was where I ought to leave the car. I did not think the barrow itself would be on the skyline from there, but if I went straight uphill westwards I ought to raise it at some point, and thought I should recognise it when I did. Then it would be just a question of finding the best line to it. I took one more look at the general picture and then drove on.

I was in the right lane. It did all the right things. For a moment I forgot my apprehensions in the curious, incredulous pleasure I always get from the successful application of the one-inch map on the spot. Then I began looking for the elbow. The ground on my left ran up in a line of rounded downs, only I did not think they called them downs in these parts, and in any case they could not be made of chalk, which all proper downs should be. Wolds, perhaps. They were a darker green and less dramatic than chalk downs. And here was the elbow, almost a hairpin, where a little valley came sharply down across the line of the road, and the road turned in to avoid the deeper, wetter part of it. There were no hedges here, only fences of staked wire, and at places a strip of turf between the wire and the tarmac. As a parking place it was a natural. I bumped up on to the turf and got out and locked the car. Then I looked up to where I had to go.

The weather had changed now. It was still warm enough, but there was cloud everywhere, and the whole world looked darker, so that the hills threatened instead of beckoned. My mood changed again abruptly, the mild excitement of exploration left me, and there was nothing but the dark summit above me and the prospect of almost certain unhappiness. I got over the fence and started walking. I did not think it would rain, but if it did, it would not matter. To some extent I was dressed for it, and in any case physical discomfort was the least I was afraid of.

I went up steadily, making not for the highest point,

but for the nearest skyline. The barrow was not on the main ridge but, where they so often built them, on the shoulder of a spur jutting out into the western valley. I reckoned that wherever I gained the ridge, I ought to be able to see it. I fancied it was still a bit northwards, in which case I could follow the ridge and then go out along the spur towards it. I felt the first moisture on my face just before I got to the top, but it was not rain so much as a heavily charged mist. It condensed on the ground, and on my face and clothes as I walked, but in the air it was no more than a creeping vapour. It darkened the air and blurred the edges of things, but did not hide anything. I saw the barrow almost at once.

As I had thought, it was still some way north of me. The top of the spur was only slightly lower than the general run of the main ridge, and I was already level with it. Seen from here the barrow was not nearly so conspicuous as it was from the other side, but it was quite unmistakable. The chalk can sometimes weather naturally into curiously artificial shapes, but these hills were different and the flattened dome of the tumulus stood up from the natural line as decisively man-made as a steeple. I turned, taking the wet air on my left cheek, and began walking along the undulating line of the ridge towards the base of the spur.

I was nearly there when I looked at my watch and found it was later than I had thought. I had told Julia I should be there before three, but I had been taking my time ever since I left the pub, and it was already past half-past-two. Still, another quarter of an hour's walking would get me there. I could in any case keep to my time, but she had said she would be there about three, and I could not bear the thought that she might get there before me and have to wait even for a short time. I felt sure she had never voluntarily kept anyone waiting in her life. It was almost level going now, and I could go faster, even in that soft dampness, without getting into a sweat inside my clothes.

The spur did in fact slope very gently down from the ridge to the barrow, but beyond the barrow it plunged fairly steeply, and I could see nothing of the farm or the ground between until I came to the barrow itself. Then I went cautiously. There was the usual ditch, silted up over the ages but still traceable, round the central mound, and I went down into it and moved round the side of the tumulus rather than showing myself on the top. I remembered how, seen from the farm, it stood up against the sky, and I had the feeling of eyes watching the hill, just as I had had the feeling of ears listening over the phone. And Julia had plainly meant me to be careful. I came round into the western side of the ditch, with the hump of the barrow behind me, and then walked to the lip and looked over.

The farm looked surprisingly close but, even with its blatant modern buildings, somehow huddled and secretive under the dark sky and the great curve of the hill. Half way between us, just where the ground started to rise sharply, a small figure moved steadily up towards me. I had not consciously taken note of Julia's walk as I had of Beth's, but I knew it at once, if only because it was so different. It seemed quite unhurried, and had none of Beth's physical ebullience, but there was nothing casual in it. For all its gentleness of movement, it was effective and purposeful. Even on the slope of the hill she was walking a good pace. I still did not show myself, even to her. In any case, I did not see her look up towards me. I stood there with my head just over the turf rim, watching her come up towards me, and full of a longing more intense and immediate than I had ever supposed possible.

Right up to the end she did not look up, and even if she had, I do not know whether she could have seen me. But I could not have her find me like that, watching her out of hiding, because it is a thing you are never supposed to do to people, even though she must have known that if

I was there at all I should have seen her by now. I walked back in the ditch to the other side of the barrow, and stood there, waiting for her head to show up over the rim. Now that I did not have her there in front of me, the whole weight of my apprehension came down on me again, and this time it was not something future and ill defined, but immediate and personal, so that I was conscious of an instinct, somewhere down inside me, to turn and run before she saw me. But of course I did not run. I stood there, with the wet air drifting on to my face, until suddenly she was there in the ditch beside me, and I saw at once that she was as apprehensive as I was.

She said, 'Thank you for coming. It's an awful place to bring you, but I often come up here, and nobody will take any notice. Where's your car? Down at the bottom?'

The extraordinary thing was the way she spoke in the standard phrases of polite apology, and yet left the assumption there, in full view, that we were in some sense conspirators, deliberately avoiding observation. It was as if she had left a jealous husband down there at the farm and come up here to talk to me about the weather. And yet we both knew that there was something down there that needed explaining, in a way a jealous husband does not, and that now we were both here, the thing had to be explained. It occurred to me suddenly that she was as unwilling to face explanations as I was, and this gave me, almost for the first time, a breathless moment of something like hope.

I said, 'Yes, down at the hairpin,' and she nodded and said, 'I know,' and then we just stood there looking at each other. The moisture stood in beads on her almost white skin. I wondered what there was in that face to be all that I had ever wanted and more that I had not even imagined. I said, 'I love you, Julia.' It was a very truncated version of what I had meant to say, but it was all I could find to say at the moment.

She frowned, not with anger, but with a sort of indignant

49

incomprehension. 'But why,' she said, 'why? No one else does.' I do not suppose for a moment that that was what she really wanted to say either, but we were talking in a sort of shorthand. People do, of course, in moments of stress, especially lovers. Tristan and Isolde do it, and people say how ridiculous Wagner's dialogue is, which in most cases is right, but not in this.

I was indignant myself now, because after all this was the crux, this was where the injustice lay, and I was still full of a sense of injustice. I said, 'But don't you want me to love you?' I could not believe that a love as big as mine could be of no importance to anyone. Then I saw that the white, upturned face was clouded over with unhappiness, and all the indignation went out of me, and I said, 'Oh, Julia, I'm so sorry. I didn't mean—'

But she smiled and said, 'No, don't apologise,' and we both laughed, and I was more in love with her than ever.

CHAPTER SIX

At this stage all I felt was relief. However little we had actually said to each other, I thought we had established the position between us. I had told her I loved her, and at least she had not said that I made her sick or she loved another, or given me any of the classic and unanswerable checks. I still could not believe that, so long as this was so, anything else really mattered. The idiotic optimism of early love possessed me completely. I knew there were practical difficulties, but they were away down at the bottom of the hill, and she was up here with me, and we were laughing together at nothing in particular, just as we had originally laughed at Jubilee Creams.

All the same, I had to know what the difficulties were. Or rather, I knew pretty well what they were, but I had to know how she saw them. I started from the one thing she had already promised to explain. I said, 'Why the secrecy, Julia?'

We were still standing there facing each other, but she did not want this. She took me by the arm and turned me, and we walked slowly back the way I had come. She still kept a hand on my arm. I remembered Charlie's grabbing hand and my desperate desire to get away from it. I did not want to get away from Julia's hand. I would not lay a finger on her, not yet, but I wanted her to go on holding me, however lightly. She did, in fact, until we came round to the other side of the barrow. Her fingers worked very slightly on my arm, as if she was trying unconsciously to communicate what she did not want to put into words.

Then she let her hand fall and said, 'Come on, let's walk. It's easier than standing still.' We started to walk, slowly and side by side, up the slight slope that led to the top of the ridge. She said, 'It's Charlie mainly. Beth, too, to some extent, but that's different. Beth doesn't matter. Charlie's not normal. You must have seen that?'

'I saw there was something, yes. And Beth told me about him, too.'

She turned her head and looked at me very directly for a moment. Then she looked ahead again. She said, 'What did Beth say?' I told her, softening Beth's wording a little, and she nodded. 'That's right,' she said. 'And you see, it makes him – I don't know, suspicious almost, very watchful, anyway. It would, you see. His mind's clear enough, and I think he's always wondering what people are thinking and saying about him, and what they are going to do with him. It must be hell, when you think, poor Charlie. But

51

it makes him very difficult – I mean, even when he's behaving quite normally. He's always – on the watch, do you see? With me, especially.'

'Hence the outside telephone calls?'

She said, 'Oh dear, I was afraid you'd notice. But that's it, yes.'

'Is there an extension he can listen on?'

'No, thank goodness. He would, I think, if there was. But the phone's in the hall, at the bottom of the stairs. You didn't go upstairs, but there's a sort of gallery at the top, with the rooms opening out of it. If anyone's up there, they can hear what anyone's saying on the phone. And of course you can't tell whether anyone's up there or not.'

I had a sudden picture of a pale, sharp face in a shadowy gallery, holding just back from the banisters, listening. I knew I had been right to be frightened. I wondered if Julia knew how frightening he was. I did not think she did. He was poor Charlie, being difficult, and she was used to him and fond of him. Above all, she was responsible for him. I said, 'But we never mentioned Charlie. The first time you rang, I didn't even know he existed.'

'No, but you're a new person. An outsider, do you see? New people worry him. He'd wonder what you were up to. Not you especially, I mean – anyone.'

I said, 'He probably knows what I'm up to. I think Beth does.'

She said, 'Oh, no.' There was such an appalling distress in it that I felt an almost physical shrinking, as if I had seen someone knocked down by a car. 'Why should he?' she said. 'You haven't said anything. We've hardly seen each other. Beth might, I suppose. Beth would be – I don't know, jealous, I suppose.' The distress had gone now, leaving only a sort of sour distaste. It did not make me feel any happier.

I said, 'To hell with Beth. No, I'm sorry, she's your sister. But let's leave Beth out of it, can't we?'

'Beth's very attractive. She's my mother all over again.'

'She's all of that,' I said. 'When I want a night out on the tiles, Beth will do fine. But that wasn't what I came for.'

She said, 'I don't know why you did come. No, that's not true. I always have known, right from the start. But I – I don't know, I couldn't take it seriously, I suppose. It's never happened with anyone before, and I really hadn't thought about it.'

I had not meant to touch her, but I did. I caught her by the arm and swung her round to face me. I said, 'Then for God's sake start thinking about it. And taking it seriously. I do. More seriously than I've ever taken anything.'

She stood staring up at me, and I suddenly saw that she was frightened. But she did not lose control, not for a moment. She put a hand up, quite gently, and took my hand from her arm, and turned away from me. For a moment she stood looking up at the dark skyline above us. Then she started walking slowly again, and I walked with her. There was nothing else I could do. There was nothing I could say, either. It was up to her now.

After a bit she said, 'Look, Ian. At least don't think I'm not taking this seriously – you, I mean, and what you say about me. I do take things seriously, and people. I'm what they call a serious person. I can't help it. My father was the same. There's no particular virtue in it, and it doesn't necessarily do much good. But I can't by-pass people. They worry me. You worry me, if that's any comfort to you. But I've got other people to worry about as well. You know that.'

I said, 'Isn't it time you started worrying about yourself?' I knew it was wrong as soon as I had said it. It was wrong because it was not honest, and that would not do with her. It was not herself I wanted her to worry about, it was me, and she had already given me that. She stopped just for a moment and looked at me, a careful, considering look.

She said, 'About my future, what's going to happen to me? "Earthlier happy is the rose distilled," that sort of thing? I've thought about it, of course. Only I never thought the question would arise in an acute form. I mean in a way involving somebody else's happiness as well as my own. I'm not unhappy, you know, as I am. I'm worried, yes. I always have been, as long as I can remember. But I'm not unhappy. Do you want me to be?'

'Could I make you unhappy?' I said. It was a question I ought not to have asked, but I could not help asking it. The trouble with her was that if you asked her a question, you got a true answer, and you have to be very careful with people like that. If you meet one, that is. There are not many of them. But the temptation is enormous. It is the old, self-destructive urge that has always driven men to try oracles and other things they would have done better to leave alone.

She said, 'Yes, I think you could. I hope you won't. No one wants to be unhappy.'

We walked on in silence for a long time after that. I had got what I had asked for, and it had not done me much good. It is an appalling thing for a man in love to be brought face to face with his own egotism. When we got to the ridge, we stopped, with that strange luminous darkness all round us and the dark country spread out below. She said, 'I'd better be going back. I don't generally stay out very long. I just come up here for the walk, and to get on top of things for a bit.'

I said, 'All right. I'll walk back with you to the barrow, if I may.'

She said, 'Of course,' and we turned and went down the slope again. We did not say anything all the way.

When we got to the barrow, she said, 'What are you going to do, Ian?'

'I don't know,' I said. 'Let me think about it, will you?'

She said, 'Of course,' again, and turned and walked over the rim of the ditch where I could not follow her. I waited until she had been gone some time. I thought if anyone had been watching for her re-appearance, they would leave their watching once they saw her coming safely down the hill. Even if they went on watching, it would be her they would be looking at, not the barrow she had left. When I judged she would be well down the hill, I put my head cautiously over the rim of the ditch.

There was nothing to see, of course, but what I might expect to see. The farm still huddled under the hill and Julia, the only moving thing in the landscape, walked steadily towards it. The house looked very dark and she looked very small, like Childe Roland coming to his tower, and it made an attractive picture, but I knew it was as false as hell. If I could have told myself that she was leaving her happiness with me on the hill-top and going back to her unhappiness in the dark valley, I should have been happier myself, but this agreeably standardised situation did not exist, and I knew it. And yet I believed passionately in the possibility of her happiness with me, and for the second time the monstrous injustice of the thing overwhelmed me with a sort of savage bitterness. Only this time the bitterness was concentrated and personal. I bobbed back into the ditch again, cursing the ludicrous furtiveness of it all, and started on the long walk back to my car.

All the way to the ridge, and while I walked southwards along it, I was making up my mind to what seemed the only thing I could do. I knew I had to get out, go back to London and take my misery with me. There was enough here already without my adding to it. In theory I ought to be able to do what is called burying myself in my work, but I wondered if anyone had ever really tried this when his work was writing fiction, and he was as inexperienced at it as I was. I could not see myself doing it for a moment. I supposed I could bury myself in biscuits. The machine would no doubt absorb me quickly enough once I put my head in the trap. But whatever I did when I got there, it seemed I had to go. I thought if things changed here, Julia could get in touch with me again. I could ask her to, anyhow, before I went. I did not specify to myself in what way things might change, but I knew what I meant.

This took me on to the down slope on the far side of the ridge, heading down towards the car. I could not see the car yet, or not for certain, but I knew where it was. I saw it clearly a few minutes later, and when I saw it, I saw that there was another car parked just behind it. I wondered if I was going to be in trouble with a farmer, but I could not see I had done anything to deserve it, except climb over one fence. Anyhow, for all I knew the second car was nothing to do with me at all. Somebody else might have business there, and it was an obvious place to park. Only I could not see anybody about, just the car sitting there, and it did not look like a farmer's car. As I got closer, the second car was masked by mine, and right up to the last the explanation did not occur to me. Then I came round mine and got a clear view of the other one, and at the same moment the driving door swung open and Beth got out and stood there watching me as I came towards her. So there were eyes on this side of the hill as well.

At least she did not expect me to be glad to see her, and did not even try to pretend she did. She looked at me from under her eyebrows with a sort of obstinate defiance, like a child caught in the act and determined to brazen it out. But she was not a child, and there was more in it than that. She had not been caught in anything. She had waited there deliberately to meet me. She could have got away, probably unseen and certainly unrecognised, long after she had seen all she wanted to see. That she had seen it I had no doubt. Julia and I had come well over the skyline, and apart from the intrinsic probabilities, I had no doubt Beth knew her sister's walk as well as I knew hers. This was an act of war, and I treated it as such from the start. I said, 'What do you want?'

She said, 'I wanted to know what you were up to.'

The fact that I had just used this phrase to Julia did not make me like it any better. I said, 'That was what you did want when you followed me here. I imagine you did follow me here?'

'In a way, yes. I was late out of town and saw you ahead of me. I stopped and let you go ahead. I assumed you were coming to the farm, and didn't want to look as if I had been following you. Then when I got home, I saw your car wasn't there, and I wondered where you'd got to. There are only the two turnings, and they both come round in a loop ultimately. So I came out and explored a bit, and here you were. Your car, anyway.'

'All right,' I said, 'you wanted to see what I was up to. Am I supposed to feel flattered?'

'You should, but I don't expect you will. There aren't many men I'd have to follow.'

It was true, too, that was the damnable thing, and I knew it even as I stood there wanting to wring her neck. For straight attraction I had never seen anything like her. It made me angrier than ever. I said, 'Well, you know what I was up to, or I assume you do. What do you want now? You must want something, or you wouldn't have stayed.'

'I want to talk to you. Shall we sit in my car or yours? Or if you like we can each sit in our own car and talk between them. They're close enough. But I must say that seems to be carrying indignation a bit far.'

I went to my car and unlocked it and got into the driving seat. Then I opened the other door and said, 'All right, come on.' After all, she had already been in my car once. That was a real consideration, because that was the way I felt about her, as if she was a sort of immediate physical threat to be avoided, like an influenza germ. She smiled and

57

came over and settled herself in very comfortably. She was much more sure of herself now.

Then she turned and looked at me. She was no longer smiling. The calculation I had seen before was back in her face, the more recognisable because she was almost visibly puzzled. She said, 'So it is Jule?'

'Julia,' I said. 'I can't bear Jule. All right, yes, it is.'

'That's really why you came here?' If there had been the slightest hint of derision in it, I believe I should have hit her, but I did not think there was. It was something she could hardly believe, but it did not strike her as funny. I simply nodded, and she nodded in reply and looked away from me, staring out through the windscreen as if she was still trying to take it in.

After a bit she said, 'Mac, it's no good, you know.'

'That's why I'm going away,' I said. I had not until that moment finally committed myself to going away, but now I knew I had to. It was something to do with my talking to Beth about it, though I could not be quite sure why that made any difference.

'You are going away?'

'Yes.'

'And not coming back?'

'I don't know,' I said. 'That would depend on Julia.'

She nodded again, and went on staring through the windscreen. Then she said, 'It's funny, really, I suppose. Here's all the local yeomanry and squirearchy running round after me with their little tongues hanging out, and none of them knowing Jule's there, and then the first man I could bear to be seen dead with turns out to be Jule's man. It takes a bit of getting used to, you know.'

'You'll get used to it,' I said. 'You're not in love with me, after all. It's mostly perversity, because I happen in the circumstances to be armed against you.'

She said nothing to that. She still seemed to be thinking. After a bit she said, 'Oh, well—' and opened the door and got out. She did not shut it. She held it open and stood there, stooping slightly and peering in at me. She said, 'If Charlie knew, you certainly couldn't come here. You know that, don't you? That would fairly settle it.'

I said, 'How could Charlie know?'

She looked at me for a moment. 'How indeed?' she said. Then she shut the door and walked across to her car.

CHAPTER SEVEN

When the phone rang, I ran across the sitting-room so quickly that I knocked over a coffee-table and barked my shin doing it. I crouched there, holding the receiver with one hand and rubbing my shin with the other. But it was only Jimmy. He said, 'Mac? Mac, where the hell have you been? I've been trying to get hold of you for days. I wish you wouldn't rush off like that without telling me.'

I said, 'Sorry. I didn't know I had to report my comings and goings.'

There was a pause. Then he said, 'Look, Mac. I'm not in this for fun. Maybe you are, I wouldn't know. But I'm here to earn my living, and selling your work is one of my ways of doing it. I might even do you a bit of good at the same time, of course, but that's only incidental.'

'All right,' I said. 'I was being bloody. Sorry. What's the trouble?' I stopped rubbing my shin and sat down to listen.

'No trouble,' he said, 'or not what I call trouble. I've been in touch with a man called Hardacre. He does radio and television scripts. You very likely wouldn't have heard of him, but he's quite well known in his own line. He wants to do a script based on Jennifer.' Jennifer was our shorthand for my first book. 'I said yes, if you could collaborate. He hummed and hawed a bit, but finally said all right, and I said I'd discuss it with you and let him know. That was four days ago, and I've been trying to find you ever since.'

I said, 'Sorry,' again. 'I did go off rather suddenly, and I've been a bit occupied.'

'All right, all right,' he said. 'I don't want to know about your love-life. But now you're with us again, you will do this, won't you? It would be marvellous experience for you, especially with a man who knows his stuff like that. Only you'll have to play ball with him. I mean, I don't know about the money side yet, but so far as the work's concerned, he'd be senior partner.'

I was still angry because it was only Jimmy who had phoned, and I had hurt myself getting to answer him. I had been waiting three days for the bell to ring, but it had not rung at all. No one had phoned me. I suppose in fact all the people who might have had tried several times and then given up trying. The person I had hoped would ring hadn't tried. And now it was Jimmy, with news I had every reason to be grateful for, and I could not cope with him or his news at all. I said, 'What would be involved? And when should I have to do it, do you know?'

'Good God, I don't know. You'd have to fix that up with Hardacre, I should think. All I want at this stage is your agreement to do the thing at all. Then I can get on and discuss terms with him, or his agent if he's got one. You will do it, won't you?'

The whole thing appalled me. I did not want to work, least of all with anyone else, and I did not want to leave the flat more than I could help in case anyone phoned. I wanted to be alone with what I had in my mind, and I could not bear to have it interfered with. I sat there with the receiver to my ear, wondering what to say, until Jimmy said, 'Mac? Mac, are you all right? What in God's name's come over you? Here's somebody coming after you instead of you going after them, and a whole new line opening up if only you'll try. You ought to jump at it.'

I said, 'Sorry, Jimmy.' I seemed to spend half my time telling him I was sorry. 'All right, yes, you go ahead and fix it up. Then I'll talk to this chap and find out what's involved.'

This time it was Jimmy who did not reply. There was quite a long silence. When he spoke, his voice had an edgy, cautious note in it I had not heard before. He said, 'This will be a contract, Mac. I said, you'll have to play ball with him. I don't want—'

'All right, all right,' I said. I knew I had no alternative. I knew I was lucky. I even knew, in the more rational part of my mind, that it might be very good for me. I still did not want it. 'I told you,' I said, 'go ahead and fix it up. I won't let you down.'

Jimmy said, 'All right, Mac,' but he did not sound very happy. Then he said, 'Look, it's some time since we met. Let's lunch some time, shall we, and we can talk things over. Can you manage a day soon?' He knew I never had many engagements, and he knew I knew that. He was worried about me, and that too I could not bear.

I nearly said I was sorry again, but I stopped myself. I put on a more cheerful tone. It sounded horribly spritely. 'Fine,' I said, 'I'd like that. Some day next week?' It was only Tuesday now. At least it put the whole thing ahead a bit.

Once more there was a very short silence. Then he said, 'All right. What about Monday? I can manage Monday.'

I said, 'Fine,' and we got ourselves disentangled and he rang off. I put the receiver down and sat back in the chair. I started rubbing my leg again. It had been quite a knock. Then I went and stood the coffee-table up and put back the things which had been on it. There was nothing breakable, only books and papers. It was only my skin that was damaged, and that would mend. I went back to the chair and sat down again, thinking about Julia.

I had seen her once more before I left. It had been at the farm, and we had had only a moment or two to ourselves. I had come out to my car, and she came out to see me off. Charlie was away upstairs somewhere. I did not know where Beth was. She had said good-bye and stayed indoors, but she was probably watching us. Julia said, 'Ian, you will be all right – will you?'

She was worried about me. I had become another of her responsibilities. Pity may be akin to love, I do not know, but a sense of responsibility generally has a dash of resentment in it, at least with most people, and I was too full of my own unhappiness to make distinctions. I said, 'I suppose so. Will you ring me some time? Don't worry about coins for the box, just reverse charges. I know you can't phone from the house.'

She said, 'I don't know. What would there be to say?'

'I don't know. There might be something. You might have to come to London. You must sometimes. Promise me you'll see me if you do.'

She shook her head, not so much at me as at her own thoughts. 'I might, I suppose. But don't count on it, Ian, please. You mustn't count on anything at all. You do understand that?' She was reasoning with me now, as if I was being awkward about things, and this was the woman I wanted, for a start, to get hold of and kiss until we were both breathless.

I nodded and got into the car. 'Oh, I understand,' I said. 'Good-bye, then.'

She said, 'Good-bye, Ian.' We did not touch each other at all. Beth must have been disappointed.

So I had promised to be reasonable and not count on anything, and so I had been, as reasonable as could be expected, and if I chose to spend a certain amount of time waiting for the phone to ring, that was up to me and did no one else any harm that I could see. But now here was this man Hardacre, and Jimmy doing his damnedest to promote my career in literature, and I had to make up my mind between the perfectly reasonable thing they wanted me to do and the unreasonable thing I wanted to do myself. I did not care in the least about Hardacre, but I felt guilty about Jimmy, and I resented very much the fact that I had to feel guilty about him when in fact the decision to be made was a purely private one.

But the bad thing was that there was really no decision to be made. There was nothing I could do at all. There was just a continuing and intolerable emptiness, and nothing I could do could fill it. The Hardacre job would happen, automatically and inevitably, because there was nothing to get in its way, but it would not fill the emptiness. I did not see how things could go on like that, but so far as the external facts went they could, indefinitely.

For want of anything better to do, I got out a copy of Jennifer and started reading it. It seemed to have no connection with anything in my present mind at all, and it was only three years since I had written it. It was clever of Jimmy to cut me in on the script-writing, but Hardacre must know more about the book than I did, and of course he knew a whole lot more about writing scripts. He must have found something in the book to make him want to do it, but I could not see what it could be. There was nothing in it for me now, nothing at all. I only hoped that when we did talk, he and I could find something to talk about.

There were two more phone-calls that day, neither of them of any importance, but at least I took them without hurting myself or knocking the furniture over. At about eleven on the Thursday morning the bell rang again, and it was a man's voice, deep but very quiet-spoken. I had certainly never heard it before, but there was something in it that set my heart going. I had the explanation at once. He said, 'We haven't met. My name's Mellors. I think you know my brother's family.' It was the family voice, of course. This was the colonel at Uppishley. Neither Charlie nor Beth sounded the least like it, but they were straight out of the other side of the family. Julia would have taken her trick of speech from her father as well as the physical qualities of the voice.

I said, 'Yes, of course.' I wondered what the hell he wanted, but at least it was a connection. For better or worse, I was no longer hanging in a void. 'As a matter of fact,' I said, 'I fancy we did see each other once, in a lane not far from your house. I was parked in a gateway, and you came past in your car.'

I think he smiled. At least there was a touch of amusement in his voice but he was also slightly at a loss. Whatever had put him on to me now, of course he had identified me as the man he had seen that morning in the lane. The car alone would do that. But he had not expected me to have identified him, still less, even if I had, to say so. He said, 'That's right. I remembered you when my niece mentioned you.' He did not say which niece. I thought Julia might or might not have described me, but Beth would certainly have described the car. He said, 'I didn't know—'

I said, 'I was looking for people of your name.' I did not want to prevaricate with the colonel any more than I did with Julia.

'I see,' he said. He sounded as if he did see, too, but now he was perfectly serious about it. His voice had this same considering quality I had seen in his face and knew by heart in Julia's. 'Well,' he said, 'I don't know – I wondered, if you had got nothing better to do, whether you would care to have lunch with me.'

'I'd like that very much.'

'Would you?' he said. It was a perfectly conventional phrase, but he did in fact sound a little surprised, as if he wondered if I knew what I was letting myself in for. I did not, of course, but I wanted to. Above all, it was a connection, something to take hold of in the void. 'Good. Well, will you come to my club?' He told me which one, but I could have guessed it before he told me. 'Say a quarter to one?'

'That will be fine,' I said. 'I look forward to it.'

He said, 'Good,' again, and again he sounded very slightly puzzled. 'Well, I'll see you then.' I thanked him and he rang off.

The colonel made me feel very young and raw, but he did it in the kindest possible way, and certainly had no intention of doing it at all. When I was on my own, or even when I was with Julia, my desperation for her was its own justification, so that her failure to respond and the outside circumstances which seemed to keep us apart appeared self-evident wrongs. I could and did rail against them as irrational malignancies. In the cool light of the colonel's judgement I was not so sure. Not that he ever offered to judge me or my feelings but the light was there, and I saw myself in it unwillingly, and was a little taken aback by what I saw.

It was not until we had finished our rather stately lunch that Julia was even mentioned, and that in itself was disconcerting. I felt like a man who has screwed himself up to meet his first lion over the top of the hill and finds, when he gets there, that there is first a wide placid river to cross, and the lion is still on the far side. The colonel did not explain his invitation at all, still less apologise for it. That was all taken for granted. He had asked me to lunch and I had accepted, and there was nothing more to be said. He greeted me as if we were already reasonably well acquainted, and talked of neutral subjects all through the meal. All the same, he was considering me, all the time, in the light of what I said. He did not ask me direct questions or try in any way to elicit what I did not offer. It was as if he had

65

decided merely to meet me, and was meeting me, and would draw his own conclusions from the meeting.

This might or might not be all he had in mind, but it would not satisfy me. I had not come for a pleasant boat trip on the river. I still wanted my lion. I gave him as long as I dared, and then, when we had got to the coffee, went over on to the attack. I forget what we were talking about at the time, but I suddenly put down my cup and said, 'Does Julia know you're meeting me?'

He was not in the least disconcerted by the suddenness of the question, but the question itself obviously shocked him. He answered quickly but in his usual soft-spoken way. He said, 'Good gracious me, no.'

It was at this point that I began to feel, as I have said, young and raw. It was not only that my scale of values was so different from his. It was because I could see that in the eyes of this very reasonable man mine was the unreasonable one. I do not think I actually asked him a further question. I probably simply looked puzzled. In any case, he went on, almost at once. He said, 'No, Julia talked about you. Well, they all did. So I thought I'd have a look at you.' He smiled gently, as if apologising for the way he had put it, but I felt certain that that was exactly what he had thought. All the same, he still had some explaining to do. Even the most responsible of uncles, as the colonel obviously was, does not vet his nephews' and nieces' casual acquaintances to the extent of asking them to lunch at his club. And of course in my single-mindedness I wanted to be rated more than a casual acquaintance. I wanted to be important, and I wanted my importance admitted, even though I knew it might turn out to be disastrously double-edged. I did not mind how young and raw I seemed. I was determined to get this out of him.

I said, 'Do you do that with everyone they meet?'

He smiled again, very gently, at the directness of my attack, but he answered me perfectly seriously, because he was, above all, not the man to meet seriousness with derision, however mild. 'No,' he said, 'of course not. But you seem to have made quite an impression on all of them.' He stopped and looked at me very directly for a moment. Then he said, 'Particularly Charlie. Charlie's taken a great fancy to you. Did you know that?'

I think if we had been walking instead of sitting at the lunch table, I should have stopped dead in my tracks. As it was, I suppose I simply caught my breath and sat there staring at him. Finally I said, 'Charlie?'

He nodded. He was considering me very carefully indeed now. 'Look,' he said, 'if you're not in a hurry, shall we go and sit somewhere a little more comfortable?'

We had both finished our coffee. I suppose I nodded. At any rate, he got up and I got up too, and he put a hand on my arm and motioned me ahead of him to the door.

CHAPTER EIGHT

I said again, 'Charlie?' We were sitting comfortably in big armchairs in one of those quiet, indeterminate rooms which the older clubs still go in for. There did not seem to be anyone else about.

He nodded. 'Yes,' he said. 'Does that surprise you?'

I thought about this, but could not come to any definite conclusion. I think the truth is that Charlie's attitude to me, simply as another person, had not seemed to me very important. It was his relation with Julia that mattered. I said, 'Well, yes, I think it does rather. I mean – we got on

67

all right, as far as I could tell, but I didn't think my being there meant much to him either way.'

'No, I can understand that. Perhaps he's just bored, poor chap. He doesn't get much male company of anything like his own age. He's very thick with Beth. It's almost as if they were twins, and in fact I find it easier to think of them as if they were. And of course he's devoted to Julia.' He gave me one of his gentle, penetrant looks. 'You know that, I expect?'

I said, 'And she to him?'

'Devoted in the strict sense, yes. She has accepted almost complete responsibility for him. She did that years ago, long before my brother died. Whether she is fond of him as a person I really can't say. It's difficult to tell in a case like that. They're completely different, of course, but they're more like parent and child than brother and sister. I never had any children myself, but I can imagine myself being devoted to a son of mine but at the same time seeing perfectly clearly that he was a bit of a bastard.'

'Is Charlie a bastard, then? I mean, when he's himself, so to speak.'

There was a look on the colonel's face which I thought I recognised, but could not at the moment place. I remembered later it was the look Julia had once had when she talked of Beth. He said, 'He may be that literally, for all I know. There wasn't much to be said for my vanished sister-in-law. She left soon after he was born, and the marriage had been on the rocks for some time before that. I think Beth was my brother's child, all right. I know he thought so, and for all her tricks, there are some definite mental resemblances. Physically, of course, they're both so much like their mother that almost anyone might have fathered them. But I know my brother didn't mean to have a son, not after Beth had been born. By then he had good reason not to want one.'

'You mean because a son was liable to be what I gather Charlie in fact is?'

'That's right. It was this thing in his damned wife's family. It only came out gradually, long after she had married him. It seems to go through the daughters to their sons.'

'I see. So Beth's all right, but a son of hers might not be?'

He waited for a moment, looking at me, wondering if I should see it for myself. Then he said, 'Or a son of Julia's either. She's her mother's child, after all, whatever she looks like.'

Because he was looking at me like that, and because I had still not got what I wanted from him, I once more went straight into the attack. 'That means nothing to me,' I said. 'I should still want to marry Julia if she would have me. She needn't have children at all if she didn't want to, surely.'

I did not think this surprised him, but I thought it was the first time he was really certain where I stood. He nodded. 'I see,' he said. 'Does Julia know how you feel?'

'Oh yes. She didn't tell you?'

'Not straight out, and of course I didn't ask her. But I did get that impression. There was something Beth said, too. Does Beth know?'

'Unfortunately, yes. Not by my choice. She worked it out, or guessed. She saw us together once. But I think she suspected something from the start. She actually said something to you?'

He frowned. He had that look of distaste on his face again. It was so like Julia it took my breath away. 'Only a hint,' he said, 'and only when we were alone. I shouldn't have taken it seriously if I hadn't gathered something of the sort from Julia herself.' He was not looking at me now. He was staring at his hands folded in his lap. Suddenly and incongruously he reminded me of Beth, that morning in the writing room at the King's Head. He was quite right.

69

There were things in common, even with Beth. Beth was still her father's child, just as Julia was her mother's. Or perhaps after all it was no more than an imitated trick. It was startling, all the same, and a little frightening. It was only Julia I wanted. So far as I was concerned, all her damned family could be at the bottom of the sea. I did not say anything. After a bit he raised his eyes and looked at me again. He said, 'I have wondered more than once what would happen when somebody went overboard for Julia.'

I said, 'You thought they might? Nobody else seemed to think so. Not even Julia herself.'

'Oh yes,' he said. 'I know Julia very well. It only needed somebody to see her properly. Or perhaps need her. That was why I wanted to see you. I hope you don't find that offensive? It's not meant to be. On the contrary.'

I said, 'Has it ever occurred to you to wonder what would happen if Julia, as you say, went overboard for some-body?'

'Of course,' he said. 'She hasn't, yet. She could, though. I told you, I know Julia very well.'

There was quite a long silence after that. We neither of us looked at each other. I was not going to speak first. We had reached the point I wanted. It was up to him now. It was the colonel who had arranged the meeting, not me. What he finally said was, 'Why did you leave Studham? You weren't there very long. I mean – you have your work to do, I know, but it wasn't that that brought you back to town?'

This was about the last question I had expected him to ask, and it brought me up short, because I did not think I knew the answer. It was no good telling the colonel I had made the great sacrifice. I did not really believe that myself now, though there had been something of that in it. In any case, I did not want to put up any sort of a front with him, even if I could do it successfully, which I doubted. I said,

'I'm not sure. I think I ran away.' He nodded. He took it perfectly seriously, but he did not say anything. He just waited for me to go on. 'I was getting nowhere with Julia,' I said. 'All I seemed to be doing was adding to her burdens. I was in a bit of a state myself, and not making myself any happier. And then there was Beth.'

'Beth's getting to know?'

'That finally, yes.' I knew this was not the whole answer, and I thought very probably he knew it too. If the colonel knew Julia, he would certainly know Beth. And anyway, the colonel was a man as well as an uncle, and he had known Beth's mother.

Whatever he knew, he did not press the point. He thought for a bit. Then he said, 'And now what? Have you done yourself any good? Running away, I mean.'

'I don't seem to have, no. I suppose running away never does do much good.'

He smiled suddenly. 'In a mental sense I don't know,' he said. 'Physically it's a different matter. I ran away from the Japs once in Burma. I ran as fast as I could. It did me all the good in the world.'

I tried to imagine this quiet, serious man against a background of jungle warfare. I found it difficult, but I did not doubt his effectiveness. I said, 'You lived to fight another day?'

'That's it. In the same war, too, that's the point. What about your work? Any good?'

I remembered, with a jolt, Mr Hardacre and his script of Jennifer. He did not seem any more real now than he had when Jimmy had first invoked him. 'Not much,' I said.

He nodded. 'I don't know much about your sort of work,' he said. He said it, again, perfectly seriously, and I blessed him for it. It is not all that common. 'But I can imagine the difficulty you find yourself in.'

I said, 'I don't really need to work.' I meant moneywise, but he brushed this aside.

'Oh, nonsense,' he said. 'Of course you've got to work.' He thought for a moment. 'You live on your own, I take it?' I nodded, and he thought a bit more. Then he said, 'Are you going to get over it, left to yourself?'

I tried to look at this reasonably. I tried, sitting there in that slightly stuffy comfort, to think what the rest of my life would be like without Julia, without even a problematic Julia at the other end of a telephone. I could not see it at all. For the matter of that, I still cannot. I had this powerful instinct not to say anything the colonel would not believe, but I could not see my way round this. 'I don't think so,' I said. I think I had been staring out of the window. There was a plane tree outside, in full leaf now. I took my eyes off it for a moment and looked at the colonel and looked away again. He was sitting quite motionless, still with his hands folded in his lap, looking at me, considering, always considering.

Finally he said, 'Then I think you had better go back. I don't know what may come of it, but give it a chance. There's nothing I can do. But you're doing no good here. Can you go back, do you think?'

'I'm not sure I can stay away.' I looked at him then, and he gave me a small smile. I think it was the first time either of us had smiled since we came into the room, and there was still no touch of ridicule in it.

'Well,' he said, 'that seems to settle it.' He looked at his hands again. He was still just smiling. 'It's funny,' he said. 'I've seen this coming in a way. I told you, I've often wondered. But I don't seem any better able to deal with it now it has come.' For a moment or two he sat there motionless. Then he took his hands away from each other and put them on the arms of his chair, and started, very slowly, to get up.

I got up too. The moment I was on my feet an enormous

72

surge of exhilaration and relief welled up in me, because I was no longer tied here, but could go, straight away, and see Julia again. I did not know what would come of it, any more than the colonel did, but I could not concern myself with that. I did not even know why I could not go before, but now could. Nothing had changed in any way I could explain, even to myself. All I knew was that before I could not go, and now I was going, and nothing else mattered at all. My mind was running ahead so fast that I had to drag myself back to the colonel, who was still standing there opposite me in that quiet room where nothing moved at all, not even the plane tree outside the window. He said, 'Well, you'll be going down, I take it?'

I said, 'Yes, I'll be going down,' but my voice sounded so odd that I saw the colonel look at me a little sharply, and I did not want to say anything more until I had it under control again.

He said, 'I'll stay here for a bit, I think. I've got some letters to write. Can you find your way out?'

'Of course,' I said. I was all right now. 'I'm very grateful to you.' I was, too, though I should have found it hard to say what for.

He said, 'Not at all. I'm glad we met.' It was all tremendously solemn and formal. We shook hands and said goodbye to each other, and I collected my things from the porter and went out into the street.

The flat, when I got back to it, looked immensely unimportant. Even the telephone had lost its capacity for good and evil, and it was difficult to believe that I had ever knocked over a table and barked my shin running to answer it. Perhaps the most curious thing is that, once I knew I was going, I was in no overwhelming hurry to go. Whenever I went, Julia would be there. It never occurred to me to think that she might turn against me, or find someone else to love instead. She was the fixed and central reference point of my life, as I suppose God is for the religious man, and the essential thing was not to feel cut off from her. To be cut off from her was intolerable, even though it was I myself who had done the cutting off. Once this self-imposed barrier was down, the need for direct and immediate contact was not imperative. I do not suppose even the most religious man prays all the time.

I thought I would drive down in the morning, and I set about my preparations in a leisurely, cheerful sort of way. There was some things I wanted in the shops, and I knew I could go out and get them with a free mind and at my convenience. I did not think, now, that the telephone would ring as soon as I had left, and even if it did, I did not think it mattered. It never occurred to me to phone Julia and tell her I was coming. Of course there was the practical difficulty of her being over-listened, though from what the colonel had said it did not sound as if the mere expectation of my return could do any harm. But I think the truth is that I did not want to tell her I was coming. I would not admit to myself the possibility that she might stop me, though I think, looking back, that that is in fact what she might have done. But my own need was so absolute that I did not want to refer it to her at all. I had to see her whether she wanted to see me or not, just as I had to love her whether or not she held out any hope of loving me in return. My need was paramount, and I could not let myself see beyond it.

I even went out that evening and bought myself dinner at a small restaurant where I did not expect to see anyone I knew. This was not because I felt furtive, but because I wanted above all to be alone with my expectation. I was not excited or actively jubilant. I was hardly there enough to be conscious of any strong and present emotion. My whole present was in abeyance, and I lived entirely in the immediate future.

I walked home placidly, choosing the quieter streets. It was quite a long way, but time meant nothing to me. It was warm suddenly, with the light clear warmth of early June that seems to come only every few years. Even the London streets reminded me of summer terms at the university, only there were no bells, or not where I was.

I had only to go home, and finish my packing, and go to bed and sleep, and then in the morning I should be off. There was plenty of time for all this, and I walked slowly. I wondered where the colonel was and what he was thinking about. I also wondered who it was he was going to write to when I left him at his club, and what he was going to write to them about. For all my utter absorption in my own feelings, I did not think it was me. He had said he could do nothing, and that meant he would do nothing. He had Julia's quality of not saying anything he did not mean. And I would not have it that the colonel had persuaded me to go back. If he had done anything, he had helped me to see, what I ought to have seen all along, that there was no reason why I should not.

I did in fact sleep very well, and the morning was mild and golden, fulfilling the promise of the night. Only my placidity had vanished in the night, and now I was in a fever to be gone. I went through all the usual processes of shutting up the flat, but in such agitation that I had to pull myself up repeatedly to make sure that I had done it all properly. It was still not nine when I carried my cases down to the garage and got the car out. By this time I was certain that the car would not start, but it started perfectly, and I settled down to the drive out of London, feeling my way cautiously against the great rush of in-coming traffic. I was calmer now. I always find driving the car a sedative rather than a stimulant.

I do not know how long I had been driving when I remembered Mr Hardacre. I know I was clear of the real town traffic and beginning to see bits of green country on both sides of me. It gave me a jolt, because that was one of the things I had meant to do, and I had forgotten to do

it. But it was only a momentary irritation at my own forget-
fulness, as if I had forgotten to put out the milk bottles or
deal with the laundry. Whatever I had to do could be done
just as well from Studham. The roads were clearer now,
and the car picked up speed.

CHAPTER NINE

They told me at the farm that Julia was out on some
business or other and that Beth and Charlie had gone down
to Grainger's. I did not know what Grainger's was, but I
was not going to ask. I knew where it was, down the brook
from the place where I had first seen Charlie. If you followed
the path along the bank, Grainger's was the only place you
could get to. Charlie had told me that, but he had not said
what it was either. I had assumed the next farm, but that
did not seem likely now. I thanked them and left the car
where it was and walked down to the brook. I thought
Julia would see the car when she got back, even if no one
bothered to tell her I had come. I did not want to come on
her unawares again, least of all in Beth's company.

It was hot on the path, and the brook ran brown and
sluggish, with the high afternoon sun striking down into
it where it was clear of trees. Even when it was as low as
this, there was quite a lot of water in it. I took off my
jacket and slung it over my arm. I did not know who would
see me first or how, because I did not know what I was
coming to, but I was at pains from now on to make my walk
look easy and casually purposive. Above all I did not want to

show the apprehension I felt. I felt apprehensive because Charlie always made me feel like that. Apart from anything else, you never knew where you were going to find him. I was not frightened of Beth except in one way, and that only when I was alone with her, which I was not going to be now. Charlie was easier, too, when Beth was there. There was not really anything to be frightened of. All the same, my easy walk and general air of pleasant anticipation were very conscious.

There was a belt of trees ahead now, reaching right across the little valley with what looked like a line of green bank under it. I wondered for a moment where the brook went, and then I came round a sloping shoulder of pasture and saw. Grainger's was a pool, an artificial pool, but so old that it looked natural. Someone at some time had put a solid earth dam across the narrow neck of the valley and planted it with trees to hold it. The water spread out into a triangular pool thirty or forty yards across. It was shallow and reedy where the brook ran into it, but under the dam it looked deep enough. It ran out through hatches in the middle of the dam. Even with the stream as low as it was, I could just hear the whisper of it from where I was. But there was no movement to be seen on the face of the pool. It lay glassy and unruffled, dark with the reflection of the green wall behind it. Nothing that I could see moved anywhere.

I walked on, wondering what I should find. Then there was a flicker of a running body on top of the dam. It looked white in the shadow of the trees and turned pale gold as it shot out into the sunlight. For a split second it hung in the air, and then it went into the water so cleanly that it hardly raised a splash. A moment later Charlie's head broke the surface and he was swimming across the pool towards me. Even from here you could see his conscious enjoyment of every movement, but that did not mask the strength and efficiency of his stroke. I walked down to the bank to meet him. He saw me when we were equally distant from the bank, he across the water and I across the grass. For a moment he lifted his face and grinned, and then he lowered it again and swam on. We came to the bank almost together.

The water was quite deep here, even close under the bank. If he had been going to climb out, he would have put his foot down at the last moment, but as it was he stayed there, treading water a yard or two from the bank, and there seemed to be plenty of water under him. He did not have to push his hair back or get the water out of his nose or eyes. His head seemed to emerge from the water as clean and unruffled as a swan's. He just tilted it back and looked up at me standing there above him on the bank. He seemed very cheerful. 'You coming in?' he said.

'I haven't got any things,' I said. 'I didn't know there was swimming to be had.'

'What, didn't you know about Grainger's? I thought—' His eyes turned sideways, and even at this distance I could see the secretive, defensive look come over his face. I think he was never sure about the past, whether what he thought had happened really had, or whether something had happened he did not know about.

I laughed, trying to re-assure him. 'You mentioned Grainger's,' I said, 'but you didn't say what it was. I thought it was the next farm or something. I didn't know about the pool. Is it cold? It looks it.'

He was cheerful again now. 'Not really,' he said. 'A bit of a shock when you go in, but it's all right after that. Look, you can borrow my trunks. I've almost finished.'

I did not want this. I was not sure why, because as a rule nothing will stop me swimming if I get the chance, and the pool looked very pleasant in the sun. I said, 'Oh, don't bother. I'll get myself something in Studham if the weather holds. You finish your swim, and I'll walk back with you.'

This seemed to upset him. For some reason he wanted

me to swim as much as I wanted not to, or not in the circumstances. 'No,' he said, 'no, you must go in. I won't be a second.' He turned over and shot across the pool to the far side. There were what looked like steps in the bank there, and he was up them and over the top of the dam before I could think of anything worth saying. I stood there, hot in the sun in my town clothes, and knowing I should only look silly if I tried to argue the thing any further. I was still looking at the place where he had disappeared when something moved at my end of the dam, and a moment later I saw Beth standing there. She was wearing some sort of white wrap, very short, but comprehensive enough from neck to hem. I could not see what she had on under it. She had nothing on her head, and her hair looked as sleek as Charlie's. She said, 'Hullo. I wondered who Charlie was talking to. When did you get in?'

'Just now. I've just walked down from the farm.'

She nodded. 'Seen Jule?' she said.

'No. No, she wasn't in.'

She scrambled down the face of the dam and came towards me over the grass. It must be swimming things she had on under her wrap. Nothing else could be as invisible as that. All I could see as she came down the bank was leg. She said, 'Are you going in?'

'I don't know. I haven't got things of my own. Charlie wants to lend me his. I must get some now I know the pool is here.'

'Oh, take his if he wants you to. You can get some of your own tomorrow. It will do you good after your drive. You look hot. Have you come down today?'

'Yes, I left early. What about you? You've been in, I take it?'

'Yes, but I might go in again. I've still got my things on. I'll see. You go, anyway.'

'All right,' I said. I still did not want to. I walked round the side of the pool and up to the end of the dam. There

79

was a steep zig-zag path on the face where she had come down. I went up it and turned left, looking for Charlie. The top of the dam was wider than I had expected, but not much of it was level. There was a level strip a few yards wide running right across from end to end, only broken in the middle by a footbridge over the hatches. Behind this, on the face away from the pool, the bank sloped very gently for another six or seven yards. This was where the trees grew. Beyond that it went down sharply to the natural level of the valley floor. The trees were well grown and in full leaf, so that there was deep shade under them. If I looked between the trunks, I could see, beyond the belt of shade, the whole stretch of the lower valley lying open to the sun, with the brook winding down through the middle of it, as if its course had never at any point been interrupted. It was a curiously impressive place, and very quiet, except for the ceaseless whisper of the water through the hatches.

I could not see Charlie anywhere on my half of the dam, but then it was on the other half I had last seen him. He had swum across the pool and gone up the face on the far side of the hatches. I walked to the footbridge, and was just going to shout to him when I saw him coming towards me in the shade of the trees. He was wearing shirt and trousers and carrying his swimming trunks in his hand. He stopped when he saw me and waited until I got to him. Then he held out the damp trunks with one hand and turned and pointed with the other down the slope of the bank he had just come from. 'You can change down there,' he said. 'There's a place. You'll see. Then you can go in off the dam. It's deep there.' He was looking at me in an eager, appraising sort of way I did not like, as if he was submitting me, in his own way and for his own purposes, to some kind of test. He said, 'You do dive?'

'In some fashion,' I said. I did not mind who saw me in swimming trunks, but I knew that when it came to the athletic graces, I could not hold a candle to Charlie. I go into the water head-first for choice, but diving is not one of my party-tricks.

He looked at me for a moment and then nodded. 'Good,' he said. 'Come when you're ready. I'll go and talk to Beth.' He went past me and over the footbridge. I think he must have been running, because I heard the hollow thud of his feet on the planks. I stood for a moment with the clammy trunks in my hand, wishing I had been firmer and wondering why I found it so hard to refuse Charlie anything. I was under the trees here, and the cool shade made even less sense of the whole business. But I knew I was committed now. There was a touch of anger in it, too. I did not like being made to feel that I was somehow on approval.

I went on down the bank and found the changing place. It was not enclosed, just a couple of corrugated iron sheets roofing a level space scooped out of the slope, with hooks on the wooden uprights to hang your clothes on and a wooden bench. I imagined, from the way Beth had come, that there was another used by the women on the other half of the dam. I took off my clothes quickly and hung them up. I took my watch off and put it in the pocket of my jacket. For a moment I stood there naked, looking at Charlie's trunks hanging by the crotch from a hook on the opposite side of the place. There was nothing offensive about them in themselves. They were plain, dark-coloured, not too scantily cut. They were damp, and they would in any case be a bit small for me, but it was not that that worried me. I just did not want to put them on. Left to myself, I should have swum naked, but I could not with Beth there. I took the trunks off the hook and stepped into them. They clung to my legs as I dragged them up, and when I got them up to my waist, their chill struck suddenly into my stomach muscles, and I shivered violently.

They looked all right. So, I knew, did I. As I say, I had not Charlie's graces, but I was a good head taller and perhaps a couple of stones heavier, and I did not carry much spare flesh. I am no great beauty, dressed or undressed, but I have nothing yet to feel ashamed of. I went back up the slope, eager now to get back into the sunlight.

From the level grass at the front of the dam the water looked further down than I had expected. It was probably not more than four or five feet below my feet, but my head was another six feet higher, and from there it looked quite a long way. The surface was an unbroken and unruffled sheet, reflecting nothing but sky. I could not see under it at all. In the corner of my eye I could see Charlie, sitting on the bank at very much the place where I had first stood to talk to him. He was sitting with his knees drawn up and his arms clasped round them. His head was forward, and he was staring fixedly at the surface of the pond. I do not think he looked at me at all, though he must have known I was there. He was quite motionless. I could not see Beth anywhere.

I walked to the edge of the dam, digging my naked toes into the short thick grass and feeling the grip. The less skilled the diver, the more he likes to be sure of his take-off. The sun was warm on my skin, and I could gladly have kept it there for a bit instead of committing myself to that chilly stillness under the dam. But I faced towards the centre of the pond, which I took to be the deepest point, and took a few deep breaths. If all this sounds more like a parachute jump than a low dive into a rustic swimming pool, I can only say that that was the way I felt about it, and I do not in the least mind admitting it. Then Beth called me suddenly from along at the other end of the dam.

She shouted, 'Mac! Mac, wait. Come over here.' Her voice sounded curiously sharp and peremptory, so that my head jerked round in her direction, and as I turned, I saw Charlie lift his head and look at her too. If I had been a second or two farther gone in my preparations, I might have been caught off balance, and finished by slithering down the bank and probably hitting the water bottom first, with my arms and legs everywhere. As it was, I simply stepped back from my toehold, and turned and walked across the bridge. I was conscious, even as I did so, of a sharp jab of relief. The sun was still warm and the cold water still a safe distance below me.

Beth had dropped her white wrap and was wearing only a two-piece swimsuit. It was dark and close fitting, but by no means a bikini. Only the unexpectedly full breasts thrust up triumphantly from inside the top of it, just as they did, given the least encouragement, from inside her ordinary clothes. Once I had turned and come over the bridge, something of the tension went out of her attitude. I suppose it is true that as I came up to her, a different sort of tension took its place. We both, it seemed quite consciously and deliberately, took fresh stock of each other's body. But that too did not last. She smiled at me. It was a perfectly friendly smile, but it invited no questions. She said, 'Come in from here with me. One, two, three and together. Will you?'

I said, 'I'd rather go in with you than have you watch me. I'm not all that graceful.'

Just for a moment she took her eyes from mine and let them run down the length of my body again. Then she brought them back and said, 'You'll do.' She turned and faced the water. 'Ready?' she said.

'Ready.' She gave the word and we went in together.

The water was cold all right, but not shattering. The thing that struck me about it, once I had my head under, was how clear it was. I was expecting something much murkier, but I suppose really there was no reason why it should be. The pool seemed to have a gravel bottom, at least at the edges, and there was nothing except the occasional swimmer to stir it up. But above all, it was deep, so deep that the bottom must be well below the natural floor of the valley. The more you considered it, the more formidable the whole work seemed. Someone must have diverted

83

the stream, or even taken it over a temporary aqueduct, and made a considerable excavation, no doubt throwing the spoil up into the dam. Even without the dam there would have been quite a pool, but with the dam as well there was a great deal of water here. I wondered who had done it, and when, and above all why.

I did not work all this out with my head under water, but I was startled by the clearness of the water and the depth of it below me, even here, and the questions formed themselves in my mind. Beth was no doubt the better diver, as Charlie was, and she surfaced well before I did. I saw her legs, sunlit in the pale yellow translucence, kicking above me as I came up, and by the time I got my head out, she was there within a few feet of me, lying back in the water and smiling at me. She was neither breathless nor dishevelled. Like Charlie, she seemed impervious to immersion, as if she was naturally amphibious. I was not. I gasped a bit, like any ordinary man plunged into cold water, and I had to push my hair back before I felt normal.

She waited there, floating and smiling, while I collected myself. The water seemed to buoy her breasts up, as the top rail of the stile had done that first morning, or perhaps it was only her swimsuit or the way she was lying back on the water. At any rate, there they were, two white curves above the flat surface, and I looked at them, compulsively, before I really looked at her face. Then I smiled back at her as well as I could, but it was still something of a rictus. I said, 'Glory, it's cold. Or don't you think so?'

'I'm afraid it is a bit,' she said. 'It never really warms up much. The sun doesn't seem to get down very far, and you soon stir the cold water up from underneath. I suppose we get used to it.'

I think it was the word 'we' that did it. At any rate, for the first time I remembered Charlie. I looked up on to the bank, but he was not there. She must have followed my eyes, because she said, 'Charlie's gone up to the house, I expect. He's due up there about now.'

I nodded. I found something unnerving in his sudden appearances and disappearances, but I could not say so. She said, 'Look, I want to show you something.' She turned over and swam easily out towards the middle of the pool, and I followed her. When we were still a little way from it, she stopped and said, 'Got your breath back?'

'Just about.'

'Come on, then.' She duck-dived easily and smoothly, heading off again towards the middle. I watched the white legs slide under, and then took a deep breath and followed her. I saw her ahead of me at once, swimming steadily through the clear water. We were no more than seven or eight feet down, and she was going no deeper. I made an effort and came alongside her, and then something large and black loomed suddenly out of the water ahead of us. It was a long narrow shape, and looked startlingly alive, as if it was moving up out of the deep water to meet us. It gave me the fright of my life. But Beth swam on steadily, and the next moment we were up to it. It was a column of rough stone, standing up out of the invisible bottom of the pool and tapering towards the top like an enormous tooth. I ran my hands over its clammy face for a moment, and then put my head up and made for the surface.

I came out into the sunlight, gasping for breath again, but with a vast sense of relief, and a moment later Beth was alongside me. I said, 'What in God's name is it?'

She laughed, but she was watching me a little closely. 'We don't know,' she said. 'No one knows. It must have been there before they dug the pool out, and they just left it, but whether it's natural or artificial you can't say. Natural, probably. It's very big at the base, if you go down that far.'

'I'll take it on trust,' I said. 'It frightened me to death.'

She laughed again. 'It's quite harmless,' she said. 'It won't come and get you. As a matter of fact—' She broke off and paddled back a few yards towards the middle. 'Come here,' she said. I swam obediently up to her. 'A bit further,' she said, 'Now – let your feet down.'

I let them down, cautiously, and the next moment I touched it. The top was flat and maybe a foot across. I got both feet on to it and balanced there, with my head just above the surface of the water.

'There you are,' she said. 'I thought you could. You're just tall enough.'

I still stood there, balancing myself in the water with my hands, looking at her while she trod water in front of me. 'So what?' I said.

She shook her head. 'Nothing, really,' she said. 'Only none of us can. Have you had enough?'

'More than enough,' I said.

'Poor Mac. Come on, then – out and get warm.'

We got out and dressed, and walked back to the house together. I walked in my town clothes, with Charlie's damp trunks dangling in my hand. I was still cold, for all the late sunlight on the path. Neither of us said much.

CHAPTER TEN

Julia said, 'I'm sorry it gave you a fright. It is a bit uncanny until one gets used to it.'

'Nothing to the fright I'd have got if Beth hadn't been there to introduce me. If I'd gone in where Charlie wanted me to, for instance. I don't think I'd actually have hit it, but I'd probably have seen it and come up with the screaming heebie-jeebies. Good for a laugh, I suppose.'

86

She said, 'Charlie wouldn't have thought of that.' She said it quickly, and there was a touch of protective indignation in it. I remembered what the colonel had said about the mother-child relation. I thought myself that that was exactly what Charlie would have thought of, but I did not say so.

Instead I said, 'What do you think it is then?'

'Well, nobody knows, of course. I've got a couple of theories, but I can't prove either of them. We don't even know who made the pool. There's no mention of it in the records. There's no local tradition either, and that puts it back quite a bit. The name Grainger's is quite recent. Grainger was a mid-nineteenth-century tenant. I should say it's eighteenth-century. There's an eighteenth-century feel about the whole thing, and some of the trees look that old. And the house was the manor then.'

'A sort of folly?'

'That's it. Gothic grottoes and all that. As for Old Mole—'

'Old Mole? That's the stone?'

'Yes, but that's only our pet name for it. Since we were children. We can't remember why, exactly. Probably a joke about a tooth, with the Hamlet quotation on top of it. Well said, old mole – you know?'

'I know. Anyway, what do you think it is?'

'Well, either they meant to leave an island in the middle—'

'With a temple?'

'That's right, or as I say a grotto. Very eighteenth-century, anyway. And then either the rock broke away while they were working, or the island was washed away gradually when they let the water in, and there was just this one spike left.'

I nodded. I said, 'Anyway, it is natural? Beth said—'

'Oh, of course it's natural. You can see if you go down. It's just a spike of natural rock that's been quarried all round. What else could it be? You don't find a megalith at the bottom of an eighteenth-century quarry.'

'You don't indeed,' I said. 'Anyway, you've seen it at the bottom and I haven't, nor do I intend to. It's too deep and too cold. What's your other theory?'

'Well, that they left it as a support for an aqueduct. I mean a temporary one, while they dug the pool out. That would be in period too, though perhaps a bit later. They knew all about aqueducts, after all. And the level's about right.'

'Yes, I thought of an aqueduct myself, even before I saw the stone. They must have taken the stream round or over while they were working. What did they do with the stone they took out – I mean, if it was a real quarrying job?'

'It was that, all right. It's all stone here if you go down a bit. Oh, that's under the dam, of course. There's old stonework on both sides of the hatches, and I bet if you dug for it, you'd find it all along the dam. A solid stone foundation, and then soil heaped on top. It makes sense.'

'Of a sort. As much as any folly ever does. I find the whole place a bit creepy myself. But then I like salt water.'

She looked at me, as she did sometimes, in a way that made my heart turn over. I could not easily put a name to it. There was a sort of apprehension in it, but an apprehension tinged with regret, as if I was a strange landscape she dared not let herself look at too long. I thought of all the places I could take her to if she would let me, and I wondered if she did not, sometimes, think of them herself. All I said was, 'Do you ever swim yourself?'

She looked away from me, and when she turned back, her face was quite different. She nodded briskly. 'Of course,' she said, 'when I have time. I generally let Charlie and Beth try it out first. They're keener than I am – and younger. Then if they can persuade me that it isn't too cold, I start myself. How cold is it, in fact?'

'Adventurous, not deadly. All right so long as there's

88

a hot sun to come out into. I don't think I'd have gone in if I hadn't been made to. But I survived.'

She said, 'Who made you?' She said it a little quickly and sharply, looking at me very straight.

'Oh, Charlie,' I said. 'Well, he didn't make me, I suppose, but he wouldn't take no for an answer.'

She nodded. 'He didn't come in with you?'

'He couldn't,' I said, 'I had his trunks. I've got some of my own now.'

She laughed, but there was a touch of something like relief in it. 'Of course,' she said, 'I'd forgotten.'

'Are you going to start now, then?' I meant, start swimming with me, and she knew it and hesitated. I waited, a little breathlessly. I had just made up my mind. I knew what I wanted and what I must do. At last she said, 'I suppose so, yes.'

'Good. When? This afternoon?'

'I can't, the early part. Perhaps after tea if the weather holds. I'll see.'

'All right.' I got back into the car. I had hardly got out of it, in fact. Julia had been there, in front of the house, when I drove in, and we had just stood talking by the car. I had not seen either of the others. I said, 'Julia, you don't mind my coming back, do you?'

She stood there looking down at me. I had never seen her looking down at me before, and it was strange and rather unnerving what a difference it made. To see a woman looking down at you can tell you a lot about her. She was what I think they would at one time have called deep-bosomed. She had none of Beth's startling show-girl protuberance, just this deep, gentle curve. I thought, the swell of her bosom. All the words that came to my mind about her had this curious, almost Victorian quality, as if, like the Victorians, I felt my desire rebuked, and the stronger for being rebuked. She went on looking down at me, very searchingly, over the curve of her breasts, and that was

89

the way I wanted her to look at me, whatever else I wanted
of her. Then I thought that would be the way she looked
at Charlie, and I damned Charlie from the bottom of my
soul, even if it was not his fault, even if it was something
in his mother's family he could not help. But Julia was her
mother's child too. That was what the colonel had said.
She was her mother's child, too, whatever she looked like,
and I remembered what I had decided, only a few seconds
ago, though already it seemed in a different world. I was
nearly out of my mind with the different ways I wanted
her, but I did not believe, if once she surrendered, they
were irreconcilable. Only she had to surrender. She said,
'I don't know. I think I'd have stopped you if I could. But
I can't send you away now you're here, can I?'

I took a chance on that. I had to. It was a time for taking
chances. I said, 'You could, you know. You've only got to
say the word.'

Her eyes still held mine, but her mouth set curiously
hard, harder than I had ever seen it. I had seen that set of
the mouth before, in other women, but never in her. She
shook her head. 'No,' she said, 'don't go.' Her voice was
perfectly clear and firm, but I could hardly hear it, even
so. Then she turned and went into the house. I started the
car at once and drove off before I could see anyone else.
Whether they had seen me I did not know, any more than
I ever did, but I did not want to see them. I turned out of
the gate and headed back towards Studham.

The weather still held. I think it was hotter than ever.
I did not go near the farm at all until quite late in the
day. I did not stay in Studham either, in case anyone came
and found me there. I drove out on the far side, away from
Clandstead, and then, in the middle of a breathless afternoon, came round in a long curve and stopped a mile from
it. I took what I wanted out of the car, and locked it and
started walking. I had been at work on the map again, and
knew where I was going.

When I came out into the bottom of the valley, the sun was still high over the trees on my left. The afternoon had that hanging, timeless quality they have when the hot weather and the longest days come together. The distances were slightly hazed, as if the air was so still and thickly-scented that you could see it if you looked far enough through it. There was no sound at all except for the birds. They did not sing much, and when they did, it only deepened the silence. I went up under the western trees, stepping as carefully in the long grass as if I was walking in hard shoes over the flagged nave of a church. I was conscious simultaneously of the huge surrounding peace and my own inner excitement. It was like 'L'Apres-Midi d'un Faune' in an English landscape.

As the valley narrowed I began to hear the brook on my right, but never more than an occasional whisper. Then, just as I had when I had come down to it from above, I came round the shoulder of a slope and saw the dam, hanging right across the valley under the deep shade of its trees. It was more impressive than ever from here, only now it did not frighten me. But I went more cautiously, keeping under the trees and never taking my eyes off it as I walked. If there was anyone there, I wanted to see them before they saw me. Only the trees were so thick I had little chance of seeing anything.

I went steadily forward, but always edging my way up the side of the valley, aiming at the point where it met the end of the dam. I was still a hundred yards from it when my movement opened up a gap in the trees, and I saw, through the gap, a small figure on the slope of the dam, very white in the deep shade of the trees. I stopped where I was and stood there watching it, with my mouth slightly open and my heart thumping in my throat. I knew it was Julia, because of the dark hair and the way she held her head. She was quite naked. She was almost motionless, but not quite. Her feet did not move, but she moved her body very slightly. Her head was down, and I knew, though I could not possibly see, that she had that considering look on her face, even though there was nothing to consider but her own naked body. Then she stooped and picked something up, and the next moment she was pulling on a dark swimsuit.

I was much too far away for the sight in itself to have any quality of erotic excitement. All the same, I was excited, excited and moved, because I had seen this most guarded and private person unguarded in an intensely private moment, and I thought that for me at least one more barrier had gone down which could never quite be re-built. I could no longer see her now. I thought she must have gone over the top of the dam, and might already be in the water. Whatever she had in her mind, I knew that she would not let herself wait for me or acknowledge in any way an expectation that I should come. For myself, I had no longer any need of caution, but I did not want her even to suspect which way I had come. I went down into the valley, almost running now, jumped the brook at the narrowest place I could find (I only got one foot slightly wet) and made for what I took to be the men's dressing place on the other end of the dam. I undressed quickly and got into my new trunks. They were not very impressive, but they were the best Studham could manage, and at least they were dry and mine, and not damp and Charlie's. Then I went up on to the top of the dam and out into the sunlight, and all the magic of the afternoon came over me again.

The pool lay absolutely still, with the heavy midsummer green all round it and the great weight of sunlight pressing down on the water. Out near the centre Julia floated on her back, white arms and legs outspread and her throat and upturned face white between the dark halo of floating hair and the dark single sheath of her swimsuit. I called to her, and she turned her head and smiled at me, and for the first time since I had known her I felt completely certain that she was glad to see me. I turned sideways and dived almost along the face of the dam. I am apt to create a disturbance when I go into the water, and I did not want to swamp her in my wash. When I came up and turned back in her direction, I found her swimming slowly towards me. She had none of the athletic elegance of the others, but she looked very much at home in the water. She said, 'Hullo, which way did you come?'

'Up from below,' I said. 'I didn't want to go to the house.'

'You're very good at cross-country manoeuvres.'

'I'm a countryman really,' I said, 'despite my urban habitat. And I like using a map.'

She looked as if she was going to say something but had thought better of it. Instead she said, 'Anyhow, I'm glad you made it. Not too cold?'

'No, but I'm not staying in long.'

'Nor me. It's my first, and I want to make sure I'm warm before I go home.' She turned and swam out across the middle of the pool, and I swam after her. When I reached what I thought was the right place, I stopped swimming for a moment and let my feet down, but I touched nothing. I tried again a little farther on, but it was still no good. I swam hard after her to make up the distance I had lost. I did not want her to ask what I had been doing. We were getting up into the top end of the pool, and I had not put my feet down again when suddenly she stopped and stood up. She was a yard or two ahead of me, and the water was hardly up to her waist. When I stopped and put my feet down, I was surprised to find how deep it was, but I still had my shoulders clear and a firm bottom to stand on. She turned and we stood there a moment, both panting a little with the swim, looking at each other. She must have been standing a couple of feet higher than I was. Her hair hung in a dark swathe behind her head, and the cut of her swimsuit covered her breasts completely, but did not disguise their shape.

I said, 'I can't understand it. You are so much the most beautiful woman I've ever seen, and you say no one's told you.'

She shook her head as if the thing really puzzled her. I thought that that was what she had been considering when I had seen her for that moment up on the dam, considering her body objectively, in the way she would, and wondering what it really held for me and perhaps even for her. 'No,' she said. She turned and started to wade through the shallow water towards the bank. I swam a few strokes to bring me up on to her level and then followed her. As I stood up out of the water, the sun laid powerful hands on my still cold skin, so that for a moment it seemed as if it was the light itself I was feeling. I have never felt anything quite like it before or since. It was one of the unparalleled things that happened on that unparalleled afternoon.

We got out on to the grass and walked to where I saw she had left her towel. I had left mine up on the dam. She sat down on the spread towel, and then turned and lay on it face down, with her face resting on her folded arms and her hair spread out so that it covered her neck and shoulders. I lay down beside her on the grass, but leaning on my elbows. I wanted above anything to put out a hand and touch her hair, but I would not let myself. I said, 'It must be something special to me. A sort of personal propensity I can't resist. I know I have no defences against it.'

She said, 'I don't think I like the sound of that.' I could not see her face at all, and I could only just hear her voice, even in that absolute silence. She said, 'Like rats that ravin down their proper bane. Do you know?'

I knew it was a quotation, but I could not place it. I said, 'No?', but she shook her head very slightly as it lay on her arms.

'Never mind,' she said. 'Perhaps I'm wrong.'

For a time we lay there, with the silence and the sunlight shutting us in. We neither of us spoke, and we never touched

94

each other, not once. I did not mind how long the silence lasted. But at last she lifted her head and said, 'You know what's going to happen to us?'

'No?'

She turned her head and gave me a quick smile. 'We're going to get ourselves sunburnt,' she said. 'And anyhow it's time I was up at the house.' She rolled over and sat up, and I sat up too, and for a moment we looked at each other. She was still smiling. I was the serious one now.

'Charlie?' I said.

'That and other things.'

My enormous bitterness rose to my throat, but I could not give it words. I swallowed and said nothing. She waited for me to speak, watching me all the time, and when I did not, she said, 'Charlie's very fond of you, you know. He was very pleased and excited when you came back.'

She spoke of him as if he was an eight-year-old. There was nothing I could do. I said, 'Well, that's good,' but she was not content with this.

'Don't you see?' she said. 'It's – it could be very important.'

'Then I'm glad,' I said.

For a moment she looked at me. Then she got up. 'Come on,' she said. 'We must get dressed or we really shall be in trouble.'

I was up too by this time. I said, 'I'll go down the valley, I think. Apart from anything else, my car's that way.'

'All right,' she said. She looked stricken, but there was still nothing I could do. We said good-bye on the grass and went each to our own end of the dam.

CHAPTER ELEVEN

This time it was Beth standing in front of the house when I drove in. She came up as the car stopped and opened the door for me to get out. She said, 'What were you doing with yourself yesterday? I didn't see you all day.'

From any other person, or in any other place, I should have taken the words in their usual sense. In that sense they were true enough. I had not seen Beth all day. But with Windbarrow as it was I wondered at once if she really meant what she said. I had come up here in the morning and talked to Julia and gone away again, and in the afternoon I had come up the valley and swum with Julia at Grainger's, and gone back down the valley again. I had certainly not seen Beth or Charlie anywhere. But I wondered, all the same, if one or the other of them had not seen me at some point. It would not matter which. If Charlie had seen me, he would have told Beth. I found it difficult to believe that one of them had not. That was the feeling I had the whole time, about them and about the place.

I looked at her for a moment before I got out of the car. She looked cheerful and even slightly amused. The great thing was not to lie to her, but I did not want to say more than I need. I said, 'I was up here in fact, but I didn't see you anywhere.'

I started to climb out of the car, and she stood back, still holding the door, like a chauffeur unloading his master. Not that I had ever seen a chauffeur who looked as Beth looked at ten o'clock on a fine June morning. She was back in her skimpy summer cotton. She said, 'So what did you do? Play with my virgin sister?'

'If you mean Julia—'

She said, 'Good lord, not already, surely?'

'If you mean Julia,' I said, 'I talked to her for a moment in the morning and swam with her in the afternoon. And don't shut that door too hard. It doesn't need it.'

She did not shut it at all, in fact. Instead she got into the car herself and looked round for my swimming things. She found them in the far pocket and came out holding them. She said, 'Well, will you swim with us today? We're just going down. And Jule's out, anyway.'

'All right. But I'm in no hurry. Give the sun a chance to warm the water a bit.'

'It won't, much. Or only the top, and the top's running away all the time through the dam. But come down, anyhow, and watch us, and then when you're ready you can come in too.'

'All right,' I said again. I did not at all mind the idea of watching Beth in her two-piece, slipping in and out of the water in the strong sunlight, the less so because she counted on my interest and was pleased by it. It is part of the social code that a man should never look at a woman too obtrusively, but it rests ultimately either on her possible rejection of his admiration or on his need to conceal it from someone else. The only thing that stops him looking too obviously up her skirt when it is there to be looked up is the fear either that she will turn sideways and pull it down or that his wife (or her husband) will catch him doing it.

Neither consideration operated with Beth at Grainger's. She played up to me with the single-minded determination of a child showing off before grown-ups, and I watched her, at first, with the uninhibited concentration of a man watching a fan dancer. The only other person there was Charlie, and in this matter at least I did not mind what Charlie thought. It was only gradually, and then with a steadily growing unease, that I came to see Charlie as part of the act. I sat there on the bank, still in my clothes, and those two glistening, amphibious creatures played in the water, and I watched Beth, and Charlie watched me watching her, and I knew after a bit that he was the most excited of the three. That shifted the focus of my concentration, and the shift upset me profoundly, because I did not want to stop watching Beth and most certainly, above all else, I did not want to watch Charlie.

The sun was warm on my back now. If I was going to get undressed and into the water, it was high time I made up my mind to it. All the same, I went on sitting there, with my knees drawn up and my head forward, staring in front of me. Then, not for the first time, but for what seemed a surprisingly long time, they both disappeared under the water together. The silence fell on the pool, and the face of the water settled into a shining blank, and I found myself holding my breath, hardly daring to move, waiting for them to re-appear and wondering where and how they would do it. Because I was conscious of it, my own attitude reminded me of something. For a moment I could not place it, and then I remembered Charlie as I had first seen him, sitting motionless on the bank, waiting for the water rats. Only now it was me on the bank and Charlie somewhere under the water, and the thing was so unpleasantly topsy-turvy that I rejected it and deliberately broke out of my sitting position and got on to my knees, ready to get up and go and change.

It was as I did so that two white faces swam up out of the water and broke surface just in front of me, both perfectly at ease and smiling under their crowns of drenched golden hair. For a moment I looked from one to the other of them, utterly at a loss, and then Beth began swimming straight towards me. She reached the bank and began to climb out, but Charlie came after her and grabbed her from behind, trying to pull her back into the water. It was only horse-play of a sort I had seen between them over and over again, but now I badly wanted Beth out of the water, and as I knelt there I leant forward and reached out a hand to help her. She put up a hand and caught mine, and then Charlie's hand came up to her other shoulder and slipped the strap off it, so that half the top of her swimsuit came down, and for a moment one marvellous white breast hung there, completely uncovered, a yard or so below my down-turned face. Then he let her go and fell back into the water laughing, and she pulled the dark stuff over herself again and came up the bank to me, still smiling, but watching me all the time.

She said, 'Isn't it time you came in?' I nodded and got to my feet. Charlie was lying down there on the water, and he too was smiling up at me with his brilliant, slant-eyed smile. I felt about as competent as a Labrador faced with a pair of playful otters.

'Yes,' I said, 'all right, I'm coming.' I picked up my things and went off to the changing place at the far end of the dam. Behind me the silence was absolute, but as I turned to go along the top of the dam, I saw Beth stretched out flat on the grass, sunning herself. I did not know where Charlie was.

Even looking down from the top of the dam you could not see Old Mole. I was fairly certain I knew the line of it now, and I looked carefully, but could see nothing. I thought perhaps it was too far out, and however clear the water seemed when you were under it, it had a dense quality that threw back far more light than it let pass. I still thought Charlie had hoped I would run into it that first time, and if I had dived deep and far, as God knows I am only too apt to do off any sort of a height, I still thought I might have. Anyhow, now that I knew the thing was there, I decided it would do no harm to try for it, if only for my own satisfaction and perhaps to lay a ghost or two. The truth is, the pond still daunted me a little, and Beth's and Charlie's fishlike familiarity with it made it worse, not better.

When I came out into the sunlight again, changed and ready for the water, I saw Beth still lying where I had left her. I did not see Charlie anywhere, but I did not stop to look for him. The pool was dimpled with recent movement, and he could not be far off. I faced in what I thought to be the right direction, took three deep breaths and went in hard and deep.

The cold, even at that depth, was less than I had expected. I made no attempt to surface. Instead, when I started to lose way, I put my head down and swam on. It is always difficult to tell how far up the surface is, but I thought I was about right. It would not take me more than a couple of seconds to get my head out, and I had plenty of breath left. In fact I was a good deal deeper than I thought, because when I came to the stone, its top was well above me. The odd thing was that seen from here, as a simple massive upright, it was much less frightening than it was from above, with its blunt nose thrusting up at you out of the deep water. I stopped swimming and put my hands out to feel the surface of the stone. My right hand found only a grained sliminess, but my left came down on a human hand, which opened and got it round the wrist with a grip like a wire rope.

I jerked my hand back convulsively, but the grip held, because the owner of the gripping hand was anchored on the far side of the stone. I put my own right hand to the stone to get a purchase, and for a moment we hung there, each on our own side of the stone, pulling against each other with our locked hands. I still think it is to my credit that I kept my head. I stopped pulling suddenly, turned left-handed and swam round to the far side. The pull on my left arm took me round much faster than I could have gone of my own motion, and in a second I was on him. He was crouched there, clinging to the pillar of rock with his knees and spare hand, like a monkey half way up a tree. I closed my right hand into a fist and hit him as hard as I could.

You cannot, I suppose, hit very hard under water, but I hit him hard enough. I do not know where I hit him, but it was somewhere in the middle of the body, and even if it is not right on the mark, any fairly heavy blow on the rib-cage can have only one effect on the lungs. We shot up to the surface together. I think we were some way up before he actually let go his grip on my hand, but that was immaterial. It is your legs you use for surfacing, and we were both using our legs for all we were worth. We burst out on the top of the water simultaneously, still facing each other and not more than a few yards apart.

Individual survival was much more important at that moment than our attitude to each other. We were both mainly concerned to get our breath back. We flapped there on the water, heads back and mouths open, each aware of the gasping creature opposite him, but neither yet ready to deal with it as a problem in personal relations. I think Charlie recovered first, because when I really began to look at him, I found his eyes fixed on me with a kind of frozen consternation. God knows it was never easy to know what he was thinking, but I was certain then, and am still, that the main element in that look was surprise. I do not know exactly what it was that had surprised him. I have seen the same look of consternation on the face of a puppy when the grown dog it had been worrying has suddenly turned and nipped it. Perhaps it is the shock of finding that the ordinary laws of nature, which you know perfectly well by instinct, have not after all been suspended for your benefit. I suppose everybody has experienced a shock of that sort at some point, but most of us do not lay ourselves open to it after a certain age.

Neither of us tried to get away from the other. We just stayed there, treading water and breathing hard and staring at each other. Then Beth called from the bank, and we both turned our heads and looked at her. She said, 'Charlie! Mac! Are you all right?' Her voice sounded a little sharp, as it had when she had called me over to her end of the dam the first time I had come here.

Probably for different reasons, neither of us said anything in reply. I turned again and looked at Charlie. He was smiling at Beth, still rather a gaping smile. I thought he nodded, but he still did not say anything. Then he turned slowly and included me in the smile. I had seen him do the same thing before, but I could never make out whether he was expecting me to share whatever it was he was smiling at or smiling at my inability to share it.

It is only by a very deliberate effort of will that you do not in some degree smile back at a smile like that, and I had neither the will to resist nor indeed the absolute conviction that there was not somewhere something to smile at. I was confused in more ways than one. The moment my face changed he was off, going like an arrow in his lovely, effortless stroke to the point on the bank where Beth was standing looking at us. After a moment I turned and followed him. I swam a slow, flat breast-stroke, I suppose because I did not want to challenge comparison with him as a swimmer. If I could, I should have stayed where I was, or swum off in the opposite direction. But I had to get out of the water, and there was nothing else I could do.

I heard Beth say something to him as he clambered up the bank, but I could not hear what she said. He replied, but I could not hear him either. Whatever it was, it was a very brief exchange. By the time I got to the bank, he was gone, and Beth was waiting for me alone. For perhaps the first time that day I looked first at her face rather than her body. She was watching me as I came up to her, neither smiling nor frowning, but with a sort of watchful concentration. For a moment I looked at her just as carefully. Then

I summoned up the effort to smile at her. It was as difficult to smile at her as it had been not to smile at Charlie, but I managed it, and once more she smiled back. She said, 'Come and get warm,' and I nodded and went and lay where she had been lying, face down on the grass.

I think Beth stayed with me for a bit, but I cannot be certain. No one makes much noise moving on the grass. I hoped she would not talk to me, and she did not. I did not want to have to deal with her for the moment, and above all I did not want to have to deal with Charlie. He would be changing now in the place along the dam, because I knew he was due up at the house soon. I thought if only I could avoid talking to her, Beth would go with him, and then I should be left alone in the sun, which was what I wanted. In fact I never heard either of them. I went on lying face-down, with my head on my arms and my eyes shut, conscious all the time of the sun on my body, but with my mind as near as possible empty of thought. I may in fact have slept a little, because somewhere or other some time got away from me. When I did lift my head and look round me, there was no one about at all, and when I at last got back to my watch, I found it was a good deal later than I expected.

I knew now more than ever what I had to do. I had made up my mind to it the day before, but now I saw it more clearly than ever. I had to leave Charlie and Beth out of it altogether, not only exclude them from the calculation but as far as possible avoid seeing them, even if it meant a certain amount of rather ridiculous hide-and-seek. Julia was still her mother's daughter, as the colonel had said. She had not gone overboard for anyone yet, but she could. I thought she was already poised for the plunge, and I would have her in the water with me if I had to drown the pair of us in the process. I did not think we should drown, but it was a risk I was prepared to take. As for Charlie, Charlie could be dealt with later, and that would be up to her when I had her where I wanted her. Beth did not come into it at all.

I had to go back to the house because the car was there, but I did not think, if I went carefully, I should see anyone at that time, and in fact I did not. It was when I was half way back to Studham that I remembered I had not written to Jimmy. When I got there, I bought a picture postcard of the King's Head and put it in the post for him.

CHAPTER TWELVE

Julia said, 'Has anything happened between you and Beth?'

I did not like her asking this, but it remained true that nothing had happened, and the fact that I had decided to avoid Beth in future made it easier to say so with conviction. 'No,' I said. 'Why?' I did not ask what she thought might have happened.

'Only that she came back from Grainger's yesterday looking upset about something, and then later you came up and just got into your car and drove off. I mean, you didn't come into the house at all. I wondered.'

Just for a moment I hesitated, but I did not want to tell her anything about Charlie. It would do no good if I did, not as things were. She would have to make up her own mind about Charlie later. 'No,' I said again. 'I was down there with them, and I think I must have gone to sleep after my swim, and when I woke up, they'd gone.' I looked at her sitting there beside me on the turf. She was dressed for the heat, too, but it was not a flowery sack like Beth's.

It was almost white, and it fitted her, but lightly. We were both sunburned now. I was my usual brick-red, that would settle down, given time, into a sort of mahogany veneer. Her skin had none of the magical gold of Beth's and Charlie's, but was darkening through ivory into a sturdy, almost peasant, tan. I did not know what this dark-skinned stock was, but I thought it had come some time, however far back, from Iberia or the Mediterranean. 'I'm sorry,' I said. 'I didn't know you were at home.'

She shook her head, as if she wanted to disclaim any special interest. 'I didn't mean that,' she said. 'So long as there was no trouble.' I wondered, again, what sort of trouble she had thought there might be, but I was not going to ask.

'No trouble,' I said. 'Only I'd much rather see you up here.'

We were up on the barrow, sitting just inside the rim of the ditch. The radiant heat was even stronger up here, but the air was lighter and there was just a touch of movement in it. It was not only the air that was lighter, either. I did not know whether anyone knew we were up here, but even if they did, we could not be overlooked. Down in the valley the trees and buildings swam in the haze, and there were eyes everywhere. Above all, up here there was no water, only dry air and dry distance. I like water, especially in hot weather, but for the moment I had had enough of it.

She said, 'I like it up here, too. Only I mustn't stay long.'

'Do they know you're here?' I said. I did not say who, and she did not ask.

She said, 'I don't know. I just came straight up. Someone may have seen me. But then I often do come up here. They can't know you're here, anyhow.'

'They can. At least they can guess.' I had never told her about Beth that first time.

She lay back suddenly on the slope of the turf and put her hands over her eyes to shield them from the sun. She said, 'I suppose so.' When she spoke as quietly as that, it was very difficult to hear the exact tone of her voice, but it seemed utterly expressionless, as if she could not be bothered to feel about the thing either way. She lay with her chin tilted up, and the mouth below the crossed hands was shut so firm it looked almost hard. I moved close to her and leaned over her, looking down at that sealed, half-hidden face. I moved very quietly, because I did not want her to know that I was there looking down at her like that. I hardly dared breathe for fear she should hear how close I was. I felt hollow with longing, but that was not a mouth to be kissed unawares. There was nothing I could take, nothing at all. It was still for her to surrender. Then all at once she took her hands away, and her eyes opened wide, staring into mine.

She looked at me as if she had never seen me before in her life, or perhaps it was that she had never seen anyone as close as that and looking at her as I must have been looking at her when she opened her eyes. Her mouth opened and widened a little, like a woman in pain or in the extremity of pleasure, but her eyes never wavered from mine. She lay utterly inert, with her hands resting where they had fallen at her sides, watching me as my face came down over hers. The experts in these things make heavy going of this matter of keeping the eyes open or shut during a kiss, but the truth is that few of us have eyes that can focus effectively at that sort of range, and in any case the shape of the face is such, at least in the white races, that you cannot kiss anybody properly and look them in the eye at the same time. I have always taken this to be a dispensation of nature. When the lips are ready to take over, it is time for the mind to withdraw behind closed eyelids. At any rate, I did not look at Julia while I kissed her. It was a long, exploratory kiss, but very gentle, with her mouth passive and unresisting under mine. I was still not taking an inch more than she was ready to give.

I took my mouth from hers at last and drew back from her a little, and only then I opened my eyes and looked at her. Her eyes were still shut and her mouth still vulnerable, with the lips a little parted. Only the eyebrows were drawn down into the slightest of frowns, as if there was something here she did not altogether understand. It is the way, one of the ways, I remember her, and always shall. I leaned over to kiss her again, but as I began to move, her eyes opened and we looked at each other, and I stopped moving. Even then, with the kiss over and me there in front of her, she still had this faint look of doubt or misunderstanding. Then her lips came together, and she said, 'Well?' She said it so quietly that even in that huge silence I could only just hear her, and yet it was not a whisper, but a fully voiced sound. I have never heard another voice like it.

And yet I was at a loss, for all my engulfing tenderness. It was I who had the questions to ask. I had told her all I had to tell, not in words, but with my mouth on hers. I wanted desperately to know how it was with her, and her lips had told me nothing. For myself I had nothing more to say. However, as Rosalind says – and I have always wondered how she knew – when a lover lacks matter, the cleanliest shift is to kiss. I shook my head slightly and leaned forward to kiss her again, but she would not have this. She turned her face away and put one hand up, touching me on the cheek very lightly, but so as to keep me at a distance. She said, 'Still set on your proper bane?'

For a moment I did not understand, but then I remembered what she had said that afternoon down by the pool. It was only the day before yesterday, but it seemed much further off. 'More than ever,' I said, but I did not think that was really true. I had reached my extremity long ago. 'What about you?' I said. 'Julia, you must tell me, don't you understand? I must know. I can't go on like this.' But

I knew, even as I said it, that that was not true either. I could, only too easily, go on like that. There was nothing to save me from it.

Her frown was more pronounced now. She looked at me as if she was trying, more than ever, to get on terms with something she did not fully understand. 'I don't know,' she said. 'I'm sorry. I still don't know.'

I think if she had been more demonstrably upset, I might have found it tolerable. Or even if she had been angry with me, instead of kind and considerate and utterly honest in the way she was. Being as she was, she made me feel suddenly young and raw, as the colonel had done, and for the same reason. With the colonel I had not minded, because all I had really wanted from him had been kindness, but Julia's kindness was no good to me at all, and she was several years younger than I was. Of course every man has his moments of feeling young beside the woman he is in love with, entirely irrespective of their real ages, but that is only a momentary, hardly explicit throw-back. With Julia I had had this feeling, almost right from the start, that she was in some way older, or at least more mature, than I was, and, loving her in the desperate way I did, it was the thing about her I found hardest to bear. It was the quality which, if she had loved me in the way I wanted, would have set her apart from all other women, but in itself it was the quality which seemed to make it next to impossible that she should.

She was smiling at me now, not with any shade of derision in it, but as if we were fellow-victims of a paradox, equally at a loss and perhaps similarly ridiculous in our predicament. She lay there, this woman I wanted till I was almost out of my mind with it, smiling up at me from the green turf in the middle of that enormous sunlit silence, and if the smile had been of a just different quality, I should have taken her there and then, even a little by force if necessary. But in the face of the smile as it was I could

108

do nothing, and indeed even the physical urge was not there in me. I stayed there beside her, half sitting and half resting on one arm, utterly helpless.

She patted the grass beside her and said, 'Lie down, Ian. Lie down here beside me. No, don't touch me. Can't we just lie and be at peace for a bit? I need that so much. It's what I come up here for.'

I did what she wanted. There was nothing else I could do. But I could not let her have her peace. I said, 'You came up here to meet me. I asked you to, and you came. You must have known there's no peace for you with me around.' I was lying on my back, close to her but not touching her. We both spoke to the sky, as if we were talking to each other on some sort of celestial telephone, only I could just see her out of the corner of my eye. I could even smell whatever it was she smelt of. I was desperately aware of her physical proximity and her mental untouchability.

'But I must have peace,' she said. 'Could we never have it, I mean you and I together?'

I said, 'Good God, of course we could. It's what I want from you. It's what I've always wanted, ever since I first saw you in the train. But not like this.'

'How then?'

I knew what I had to say, but I knew that I could not say it, because it would be no use. I knew that it must not be put into words until she had committed herself so far that when it came to the point she could go only one way. For all my immediate helplessness, or perhaps just because of it, I was full of the cunning of love, as if her very honesty compelled me to an unwanted and unaccustomed deviousness. 'Not here,' I said.

I did not mean this hill-top, or the farm and the whole circle of her responsibilities, or even a world that had Beth in it. I meant the one person she had accepted an absolute responsibility for, whom I remembered, still with an almost incredulous horror, crouched like a monkey on his under-water tree, waiting to grab me if I swam into a world where he was stronger than I was. There was no peace for her and me in a world with Charlie in it. But it was for her to shut him out. There was nothing I could do but give her good reason, at last, for doing it.

For quite a long time she said nothing. I do not know whether she was working out in her own way what I had meant, and if so, what she made of it. All that happened was that she lifted her left hand and looked at her watch and said, 'I must go.'

I sat up and turned over on my elbow again, looking down at her. She was still looking straight up, and her eyes did not move, though she had only to turn them to look at me. I said, 'I'm sorry I disturbed your peace. You don't get much, God knows.'

She did not say anything to this. It was as if she had made the break and did not want to go back at all over anything that had been said. Instead she reached up a hand, blindly, still without looking at me, and pulled my head down to hers. This time her mouth came to meet mine, and for just a moment she kissed me as much as I kissed her. But not for long. The hand that had pulled me to her pushed me away again, and in my wariness I did not resist it. She still lay there, but now her eyes were shut. She said, 'Will you go now? I must go down myself in a minute or two. But leave me here just for a bit, will you?'

She spoke very quietly, and I, almost as quietly, said, 'All right,' and got up and walked round the ditch to the far side of the barrow and so out on to the slope of the spur that led up to the ridge. I walked up it steadily. There was nothing to look back for. I do not know how long she lay there before she got up and went over the rim of the ditch and down towards the farm, but I could not have seen her even when she did. All the way down the hill I was in mortal fear that I should see Beth's car standing beside mine, as I had seen it before, and it was not until I was quite far down that I convinced myself finally that it was not there. When I got to the car, I ran it quickly out on to the tarmac and made off back the way I had come, anxious to put myself on neutral ground, so that no one, seeing my car on the road, could know where I had come from. Once I was into the Studham road, I drove slowly, looking for a place to pull off it and park. I wanted to think.

I did not quite know how I was going to manage things now. It was as if, going back to those remote days of my childhood, I had had a row with my friend, but still wanted to go on seeing my adored Daphne. It was not even as if I was trying to make up to a wife unbeknownst to a jealous husband, because Julia was not the one for that sort of intrigue, and in any case I could not tell her, in so many words, that I was trying to avoid Beth and Charlie. That would involve me in too many explanations that I was not yet ready to give. She would understand my wanting to see her alone, but not my not wanting to see the others at all, or at least more than I could help. It was not going to be easy.

I am not quite sure what the connection was in my mind, but I found myself wondering whether the colonel was back at Uppishley. There was nothing to stop my calling on him now. Indeed, it would be no more than reasonable good manners if I did. Whether he would want me to I was not so sure. I had the idea that he would be for keeping out of things once he had made his reconnaissance and decided that no action was called for on his part. But I thought, nevertheless, that he might in these new circumstances be useful to me. I felt certain, now that I knew him, that Julia would see him from time to time, and from what he had said I doubted whether he saw much of the others. A complication was that I had no reason to suppose that he had since told Julia of our meeting in London. He might have, and if he had, it did not necessarily follow that she would have mentioned it to me. But I was not sure either way, and the last thing I wanted was to damage in any way the confidence I felt sure she placed in him. I believed, perhaps without very much evidence, that he was on my side.

Finally I decided that the best thing was to write and ask if I could come and see him, and at the same time to put to him straight the difficulty I was in. Then it would be up to him. If he liked to tell Julia about our London meeting, he could. If he had already told her, he could tell me so. If he had not and did not want to, he could decide whether or not, in the circumstances, he wanted to see me again. Of course what I really wanted in all this was that the colonel should in some way make it easier for me to see Julia without going to Windbarrow. I was very far from clear in my mind what I expected him to do about it. I did not see him exactly in the role of Uncle Pandarus. I think the truth is that my desperation drove me to look for help wherever I could find it, and my sense of outrageous injustice was such that I could not believe that any man of goodwill would not be ready to help me if he could. If you are looking for something to arm yourself with, righteousness is nothing to a burning sense of your own needs.

Having made up my mind, I drove back to the pub and sat down straight away to write my letter. Then I went out and posted it. I could not believe it would not reach Uppishley next day. What I did not know was whether he would be there to receive it. As I was so apt to do, I had relieved my mind by deciding on a course of action and carrying it out, but began, once it was done, to doubt whether at the end of it all I was to any real extent the better for it. The trouble was that everything I did was an almost conscious substitute for the only thing I really wanted to do, which was to go to Julia. It was not only that I wanted to go to her. As soon as I was away from her,

I became convinced that there was something solid to be gained by seeing her again. I thought of things I ought to have said and had not, or new things I could say if only she gave me the chance to say them. I talked to her almost incessantly in my own mind. It was only when I was with her that I could find next to nothing to say. I do not think this means that she was a different person from the one I was in love with. I really knew her very well, and still do. It was myself I could not deal with. I do not think love is a delusion. A man in love thinks very clearly, because his mind is wonderfully concentrated. What suffers is his capacity to act, even to his own advantage.

CHAPTER THIRTEEN

I had a note from the colonel soon after breakfast. It just said, 'Come and see me by all means. I'll expect you at eleven this morning.' He must have had my letter early and sent someone straight over. Not so long ago it would have been a groom on horseback. For all I know it may still have been, but the speed suggested a car. All I noticed was that getting a letter from the colonel seemed to improve my status with the landlord. I suppose the colonel was by way of being squire in his part of the country.

I was on my way when I realised that I did not know whether he was married or not. From what he had said I was fairly certain that he had no family, but there might still be a wife. I did not think so. I had put him down for all the world as a well-regulated bachelor, and I certainly hoped he was. I was not sure why, but I did not want another woman brought in on this. As soon as I got to the Grange, I knew I need not have worried. It was a bachelor establishment if ever I saw one, and very nice too. The room I was taken to was a pleasant combination of sitting-room, office and gunroom. It had none of the concentrated and rather desperate masculinity of the traditional den or study in a married household. There were flowers as well as tobacco smoke, and the coffee tray was a picture in itself. He poured out the coffee and sat me down and said, 'Well now, what can I do for you?'

'To be honest,' I said, 'I don't really know. But it's nice of you to see me.'

'That's all right. I'd be glad to help. It's time Julia was settled, and from what I've been able to find out you'd do all right.'

Relief and something like affection flowed over me in a warm wave. It was the tremendous ordinariness of the whole thing that I found so comforting. I did not mind if it made me feel a little silly. I had been fighting demons, consuming myself in a desperation of love and hate, and to find myself looked on as a mere matrimonial prospect did me all the good in the world. I could even see it was slightly funny. I smiled at him and said, 'I'm glad I pass muster, anyway.'

He smiled too. 'Oh yes,' he said. 'Mind you, I don't want you to think I've been hiring private detectives or anything. Just asking around a bit, you know? I don't know you well, obviously, but I can't find anything against you. So as I say, if there's anything I can do— Well, look. Suppose you tell me how things stand. It's some time since I saw you.'

I said, 'You talked of Julia's going overboard for some-one, do you remember? You said she could, but hadn't done it yet. She still hasn't, but I believe she's getting near it, and I believe it could be me she goes overboard

114

for. Only she can't let go. She's still trying to have it both ways, and still believes she can. I don't, but it's as much as my life's worth to say so. I don't want to force the issue until I feel more certain of her than I do now.'

He did not comment on this, but the question he asked showed how precisely he had understood it. He said, 'What about you and Master Charlie?'

'Julia says he's very fond of me. But then you thought so too.'

This did rouse him. His eyebrows went up and his mouth set hard. He was not looking at me now. He said, almost to himself, 'That's bad.'

I had thought it was bad, too, but I was not quite sure why I thought so, and I wanted to know why he did. 'Julia thinks it's good,' I said.

He nodded. 'So should I if I believed it. But I don't, not now. I did before, and Julia didn't. I don't now, and if Julia does, it means he's been getting at her. That's what's bad.' He looked at me. He said, 'You don't say what you think.'

'I find it very difficult to say. I can't understand him, for one thing. And I'm afraid I dislike him very much myself. Partly it's just jealousy, of course. He's the obstacle, and I resent him as such. But it's not only that. He gives me the creeps. Once at least he has really frightened me. He seems perfectly friendly. But – I don't know.' I wondered if this was really true. I wondered if, looked at in the colonel's comfortable sitting-room, this was all my bitter anger amounted to. I doubted it, but I let it stand.

The colonel had been staring in front of him, considering, in the way all the family did at times, and now he just raised his eyes and looked at me from under drawn brows. 'Care to tell me?' he said.

I thought about this, but I did not want to tell him. 'I don't think so,' I said. 'It may have been just horse-play. There's a lot of that in him. As if he was still a school-boy.'

He had dropped his eyes again, and now he nodded without looking at me. 'That's the trouble,' he said. 'You can't tell. He gets excited, you see. Well, that's the thing, of course. That's why they had to take him away from school and have to look after him as they do. But I mean – you can't tell what he's thinking in between. He does think, you see. There are no flies on him at all. And you can't tell what's just this temporary lack of control and what's something much more calculated. He acts up to it, of course. People like him always do. It's like these people who tell you, quite cheerfully, that they've got the devil of a temper – you know, as if it was something to be proud of. All right, they may be just apologising for a weakness. But they may be just preparing the ground, so that when they want to turn nasty, you'll be more likely to accept it. Only of course in his case it's much more serious than just bad temper. But the principle's the same. And there's the same difficulty. You can't tell what's an unintended outburst and what's deliberate wickedness.' He thought for a moment. Then he said, 'How much does he know, do you think?'

'About me and Julia?' He nodded. 'I don't know. To my knowledge he's seen and heard nothing to put it in his head. But I have this feeling that he sees and hears much more than he lets on. I get that feeling about the whole place. That's why I don't want to go there more than I can help. And there's Beth, too.'

He lifted his face and looked at me. 'What about Beth?' he said.

'Well, she does know. I told you that. And she might have told him something. I don't know. It's a very odd relationship. Between him and Beth, I mean. She talks about him in a perfectly detached way, poor Charlie, you know. But at times I feel they're working together somehow. Only I don't know whether she's just using him, or he's using her, or whether they really are acting in concert.'

He was still looking at me. He said, 'What's she up to, then?'

I did not like this at all, but there was no going back and no getting round the colonel. I swallowed. I don't think I was looking at him, or not very straight. 'I'm sorry,' I said. 'I think she's – well, jealous of Julia, I suppose.'

He said, 'You mean she wants you herself?'

I said again, 'I'm sorry. It sounds— All right, yes. Not seriously or permanently, of course. Just for kicks. And I suppose to put a spoke in Julia's wheel, too, if she can.'

'You needn't apologise,' he said. 'She's a natural man-trap, of course, as her mother was. What about you?'

'I haven't put a finger on her,' I said. 'But – well, it's another reason for keeping away from the place.'

'Good,' he said. 'You're an honest sort of bugger, aren't you? I like that. Of course there are women who ought to be certified in some way, so that it's agreed that whatever you do with them doesn't matter. But you can't expect a wife to see it like that. She wouldn't accept the certificate. Or most of them wouldn't.'

He was smiling now, and I smiled at him. I really liked him very much. I said, 'You haven't been married your-self?'

'No, but I've commanded a regiment in peace-time. I've seen plenty of it, all ranks from private soldier to general officer. Believe me, war's nothing to it.' He thought for a moment. He was no longer smiling. 'All the same,' he said, 'I don't see how you can stay away from Windbarrow altogether. Especially if you're not ready to tell Julia why you're staying away. And I don't see it can do any harm your seeing Charlie and Beth together. It may help to – well, bring matters to a head, I suppose. They've got to come to a head some time. About Charlie, I mean. It can't go on like this indefinitely.'

'You mean, with Julia?'

'Well, Julia's the one that matters, of course, but with

everybody really.' I was not sure what he meant, and looked it. He said, 'I mean, if things are the way we think, he's going to have to be put away some time. Not necessarily certified, but at least put somewhere where they're better qualified to look after him. And that would let Julia out. But of course as things are, she's the one who'll fight to prevent it.' He thought again for a moment. 'The trouble is, we don't really know,' he said. 'We know there was a case in the last generation. My damned sister-in-law had a brother somewhere, but it was all very carefully buried, and we can't get the details. And you see, she had gone off long before we started having trouble with Charlie. The doctor's a sensible chap. You haven't met him? He's the one who can influence Julia if anyone can. But it may not be the doctor who forces her hand in the long run. It may be the police. Let's hope not, but it could happen. But so far as you're concerned, the thing to do, surely, is not to be alone with him.' He looked at me and smiled. 'Or with Beth, if it comes to that. Whatever they cook up between them, if that's what they really do, I don't see either of them can do much harm so long as they're both there. So if you're with them and they look like separating, you separate too, from both of them. I told you, there's no harm in running away at the right time, and sometimes it's the only thing to do. Meanwhile I'll try to think if there's anything I can do.'

I said, 'You don't need me to tell you how grateful I am. Merely talking about it like this is a good thing. Cuts it all down to size, I suppose. You haven't told Julia we've met?'

'No,' he said, 'but I'm going to have to, obviously, if I'm to be of any use. If you don't mind, I'll blame you for it. I'll say you heard I existed and came and saw me, or something. So long as I tell her you're all right with me, I don't see why she should object. I won't tell her we met in London. That does sound a bit like ganging up on her, and I don't want her to think that, even if it is for her own good. Would you agree?'

'Certainly. So long as we both say the same.'

'Yes. Well, that's agreed then. And once that's cleared up, I don't see why you shouldn't meet her here. I don't mean as a sort of *maison de convenance*. I mean when she's coming here anyhow. She generally has a meal with me once a week or so, and we talk shop. Mostly it's asking me how to get round that old ass Canning. But I mean, if you joined us for the meal, she and I can have our session, and perhaps she can spare you some time afterwards.'

I think he meant the last bit to be mildly facetious, but it was no joke to me. I said, 'That would make a change, certainly,' and he looked at me sharply.

'What, always having to rush off, is she? She's not as busy as all that. Of course, there's this routine with Charlie, fixed times and all that. But it sounds as if she's making excuses. That's good. It sounds as if you've got her on the run a bit.' He was very cheerful and military about it, and once again it made me feel slightly silly but undeniably happier. 'Anyway,' he said, 'she's got the evenings, once that young monster's bedded down for the night. We'd better arrange a dinner. I'll see what I can do. You haven't asked her out in the evening yourself?'

'I didn't think she'd come. Not up to recently, anyhow.'

He made a sound which I suppose should be written 'Bah'. I did not think I had ever actually heard anyone say 'Bah', but this was surprisingly near it. 'Bah,' he said, 'you want to force her hand a bit.' I felt like a subaltern being lectured on tactics, as if he had said, 'force their hands a bit'. It occurred to me that the colonel, in this as in more professional matters, could have been a formidable campaigner in his day in spite of his essential seriousness, or perhaps because of it. He must have caught what I was thinking, because he stopped bustling and suddenly became gentle with me. 'Look,' he said, 'don't misunderstand me.

119

I know this is serious for you. If I didn't think that, I shouldn't be saying what I am. But try not to take it too tragically. It doesn't help, you know.'

I had very little resistance left in me by now. I smiled and said, 'I'll try not to,' but all the time there was a shadow on my mind which I knew the colonel's cheerfulness had not really penetrated. I knew, at the same time, that it was not his fault, but mine, because of what I had kept back. He was able, surprisingly and almost against my will, to make me feel better about Julia, but nothing was ever going to make me feel better about Charlie. But it was too late to tell him that now, and in any case I could not have brought myself to do it. All the same, I wished I had gone to see the colonel before.

We parted at the same level of cheerfulness. We did not concert plans, but it was obvious that I had better not try to see Julia again until I had given him a chance to do what he had in mind. This did not stop me wanting to. The weather still held to its almost incredible perfection, and I could not get out of my mind the afternoon when I had met her at the pool. I could not help thinking that if I went up to Grainger's from below, as I had before, and at the same time, something, if only the way I felt about her, might bring her there to meet me. It was a chance, anyway. There seemed nothing to keep me from the place now, and if she did not come, at least nothing was lost. If she came, that was all I wanted, and never mind the colonel's plans. I was not prepared to argue the thing any further. I had decided to do something later in the afternoon, and that would help me to get through the day.

As the day wore on I began to think that she was more likely to go up to the barrow than she was to go down to the pool. Especially if she had something to think about. I had no idea how quick the colonel might be to act, but if he had gone over to Windbarrow fairly soon after I had left him, the thing, for better or worse, would be done by now, and that might send her up to the barrow in the afternoon. If she went to the pool, I assumed by now, having once got the possibility into my head, that she would go with the idea of finding me there. The possibility that she might merely feel like a swim on a hot day never occurred to me. On balance I thought she was more likely to go up to the barrow, but if she went to the pool, she must not fail to find me there. The dilemma was one I had constructed entirely out of my own imagination, but I was tormented by it.

I reached a point where I could not bear to let either possibility go completely, and thought that if I could find some place where I could see the hill-face above the farm, I could watch it to see if she started up it. If after a certain time I had not seen her, I could double back and find my way to the pond. The fact that, if I did that, I was more or less bound to reach either place some time after she did never really came clearly into my mind. I adopted the plan, not because I had any clear idea how it would work out, but because it was the only thing I could bear to do. I drove out to Clanstead quite early in the afternoon, looking for my vantage point.

There was no great difficulty in finding it, such as it was. The hill stood well up over the valley and could be seen from many places well away from the farm. The trouble was – and I began to see this now and fret about it – that I had to approach either the pool or the barrow from the far side, and this meant the longest possible circle from any point facing the slope of the hill. Whichever I went to, it would take me a long time to get there. But I was committed to my wait now. I put the car in a field-gate and took up my position just inside the field. It was the same still, brilliant weather. The great slope I was looking at across the valley already showed a paler green as the sun took the moisture out of the turf, and the air between was thick with the translucent heat haze. It was a moving figure I

was watching for, a tiny figure under the great sweep of
the hill, moving steadily up it as I had once before seen
her from above. That had been under dark skies and in
what seemed a different world. I was obsessed now with a
sense of urgency, which I knew was not reasonable, but
which I could not shake off. I stood there, blinking my
eyes in the heat as if I was afraid they might not see her
properly if she did come, but however long I looked at
the hill, nothing moved on it, nothing at all.

CHAPTER FOURTEEN

I cannot say exactly how long I stayed there staring at the
hill. I know when I left, but not when I got there. The sun
got farther and farther over, but did not lose its heat. I
thought that during the early part of the afternoon Charlie
and Beth would be at Grainger's anyhow. This would mean
that Julia would not be there, or even if she was, it was no
use my going. But later I thought they would have left,
because Charlie had to be up at the house. I was not sure
when that was, but I remember coming quite suddenly to
the conclusion that the time was past. It was after that that
the dilemma really began to hurt, and I began making myself
wait another quarter of an hour by my watch. It was just
before four when I finally gave up my watch on the hill
and drove off to the place where I had left the car when
last I had walked up to Grainger's from below. I did not
look at the time again after that. I just did everything as
fast as I could. Now that I had committed myself to one

course of action, I was obsessed with the idea that I might already have left it too late.

This time when I came in sight of the dam I did not like the look of it at all. It hung there, heavy and dark, right across the valley, and had taken on its old character of something unreasonable and slightly menacing. The leaves were changing already with the early heat. They had a heavy, lifeless green that was more like late July than mid-June. I toiled up through the long grass, sweating with my mindless hurry and dry-mouthed with the heat and my long uncertainty. I was still well below the dam when the whole structure of fantasy collapsed suddenly in my mind, and I saw with perfect clarity that there was not the slightest reason to suppose that Julia would be at Grainger's at all. It was so sudden and so unarguable that I stopped and stood there, panting and dangling my swimming things in a grip so relaxed that I almost let them fall, and then felt the chill as the sweat dried off between my fingers and the bunched cloth. I waited while I got my breath back and then went on doggedly. I was without hope now, but there was nothing else I could do. At least I no longer tortured myself with the possibility that Julia might after all be up at the barrow by now. I had no reason, except my own need of her, to think that she was anywhere in particular, and I no longer believed that my need in itself could bring her to me.

I crossed the valley just below the dam as I had done before, but made much less of a job of jumping the brook, so that I got one shoe full of water and the trouser leg wet almost up to the knee. I remember I got a sort of backhand satisfaction out of this small physical upset, as if it confirmed and somehow rationalised my mental despair. When I came up on to the top of the dam, the picture changed again, as it had before. The pool lay flat and silent in the sunlight, and my mood dropped suddenly from an active bitterness to a blank and passive acceptance, that had curious undercurrents of relief in it. There was no one there, of course.

I went back into the trees and took off my clothes in the appointed place. They were chilly with sweat in the shade of the trees, and it was a relief to get rid of them. With the place all to myself, I could perfectly well have changed in the sunlight on top of the dam, but it never occurred to me for a moment to do it. The place imposed its own rules and ritual as firmly as a municipal swimming-bath. I put on my trunks and took my towel, and walked along the dam and over the bridge and down on to the grass on the far side of the pool. I did not even bother to spread out my towel to lie on. The grass was too limp and dry for that. I just lay flat down on it, with my head to the trees and my feet to the water. I shut my eyes and felt the sun on the skin of my upper eyelids, where it so seldom strikes. I had no particular intention of swimming. I might swim later, but it was not that I had come for. I had come to meet Julia, and I knew with an absolute certainty that she would not come now. I had no more reason for this than I had for my earlier belief that she would, but I felt equally certain of it. I am not sure I even any longer wanted her to come, because I did not know what I could say to her if she did. It was as if I had put everything I had into the anticipation of seeing her, and now that had gone, there was nothing left in me. I felt myself slipping into sleep and pulled myself back, because it was not a place I really cared to sleep in. All the same, I must at some point have gone to sleep, because I had a long and very vivid dream.

I dreamed I was with Julia on some very steep and high place. It was not like any of the places round here, except that it was bathed in the same golden light, which must have been beating on my eyelids as I slept. Right down below me, very far down, there was a sheet of water. It had the same bright light on it, and things moving about in it, and I was terrified that I might slip down into it, which I knew would be fatal. So long as I stayed up here with Julia I was all right, and I tried to take hold of her to steady myself, but I could not touch her, even though she was close beside me. When I looked down at the water again, I could see a slim golden creature swimming about in it, which I knew was Beth, but it did not look like Beth, more like a fish or some sort of water-snake, weaving about so that it made long tracks on the surface. I knew there was another creature in the water too, and if I waited for long enough it would show itself, but it stayed underneath. I did not give it a name, but it was that I was afraid of. I turned round to look at Julia, and I found she was naked, but although she was close to me, I could not see her in any detail, just the fact that she was naked. I was seized with an immediate and desperate physical need of her, but I could not get to her, and in any case I was entangled in something tight and clinging round the crotch which I could not get rid of. She did not move or speak to me, but stayed there, just out of reach, while I struggled with the obstruction. Then I knew I was beginning to wake up, and I tried to stay asleep long enough to get what I wanted, but I could not, the light was too strong on my eyes.

I drifted awake to a sense of blinding light in my eyes and acute discomfort in my loins, where my tight swimming trunks were impeding the natural physical concomitant of my dream. I put one hand over my eyes to shut out the light, and with the other I pulled the obstructing trunks away, and for a minute or two I lay there on my back, physically at ease but full of the sense of loss and urgency the dream had left in my mind. Then I took the hand away from my eyes and opened them, and saw Beth standing looking down at me. She was wearing her short white wrap, and her eyes were wide open and staring. She took them from what she was looking at and turned them to mine, and for a moment we looked into each other's eyes as she moved very slowly towards me until she stood right over me, with her feet spread almost on either side of my head. The white skirt hung wide on her golden legs, and I saw in unarguable detail that she had nothing under it. I remember putting up a hand to grab her and pull her down to me, but I doubt if my pulling had much to do with it. One of us got my trunks down to my ankles. I think it must have been her, because I do not think I ever got my shoulders off the grass at this stage, though I know I kicked one foot clear of the trunks later. She had opened her wrap wide in front, so that I could see her breasts moving as she moved, and all the time she stared down at me with those wide blue eyes and never stopped smiling, right up to the last. We neither of us said anything at all, and we did not even kiss. I did not want to talk to her or have anything to do with her as a person. She was the succubus, the merest physical embodiment of a man's dream, and I lay almost as inert as if I had been really still asleep. Even at the end she did not fall forward on to me as a woman does, but simply crouched there while I slipped out of her, and then got off me and gathered her wrap round her and was gone, still smiling as long as I could see her. I rolled over on to my face and put my head on my arms, so that I should not see her if she did come back. I do not know if she did or how long I lay there, but when at last I did turn over and sit up, there was no sign of her.

It was almost evening now, but the endless golden evening of the longest days of the year, and the air was as warm as ever. There was not a sound anywhere, and the water lay flat as a glass sheet. I wanted to wash myself, but I would no more have gone into the deep water than I would have walked naked into fire. Finally I knelt cautiously on the edge and sluiced the water over myself with my hands, and even so it struck so cold on me that I shivered and dried myself quickly with my towel. Then I walked up on to the dam, naked and carrying my wet trunks in one hand and my damp towel in the other, and went to where I had left my clothes. I did not get dressed at once, but sat there on the bench with my elbows on my knees and my head on my hands, trying not to think. Finally I roused myself and started to dress. I was just about dressed when I heard the sound from the other side of the dam. There was no mistaking the sound. Somebody had dived into the pool.

I was still barefoot, but I left my shoes and socks and bathing things where they were and went up, very cautiously, to the top of the dam. There were no sounds from the pool now, and in the vast silence I watched every movement I made and every place I put my foot down. When I got to the top, I went down on my hands and knees and edged forward like a stalking beast, inch by inch, until I could see first the far side of the pool and then, as I got higher, more and more of its surface. When I had gone far enough, I stayed there, crouching, ready to duck under the bank at the slightest danger of being seen.

Julia was floating in the middle of the pool, exactly as I had seen her that other afternoon, white skin and dark swimsuit and her dark hair floating round her head. She looked utterly at peace, as if she had come down to cool and refresh herself at the end of a long hot day. I believe her eyes were half shut, so that she might have been almost sleeping on the water. So long as she did not move, I stayed there, watching her. Then she rolled over on her face, but away from me, and swam slowly towards the far bank, where I could see her towel spread on the grass, very nearly where I had been lying not so long ago.

I pulled myself down under the bank and scrambled back to the dressing place. I put on my shoes and socks, but my hands were so unsteady that I had trouble tying the laces. Then I picked up my things and went down the face of the dam and ran as fast as I could across the valley. I must have cleared the brook at a jump this time, but I do not remember doing it. I ran till I was in the shelter of the trees, and then ran on through them, down along the side of the valley to where I had left the car. I did not worry about the noise I made now, but my feet did not make much in the soft going under the trees. The noises I made came from my mouth, because I was out of breath, and sobbing as I ran.

When I got to the car, I did not turn back the way I had come, but headed straight on. I did not know where I was going, but I wanted to get as far away from Clanstead and Studham as I could. Of course I should have to get back to Studham some time that night, but I was not likely to lose myself in that orderly English countryside, with hours of dusk ahead of me and maps in the car. I was starting to think now, but it was Beth I was thinking about, not Julia. My capacity to think coherently was limited, as was my capacity to hurt myself any further.

If I had known more about Beth as a person, it would have been easier, but I really knew her very little. I had contented myself, if that was the right way of putting it, with seeing her almost entirely as a body, but I knew from glimpses I had had of it that there was a calculating mind inside that golden head, and I did not know what the mind wanted. Or rather, I had known what it wanted up to a point, but that point had now been reached, and I did not know what it would want next. Whatever it wanted, I thought it would be ruthless and unscrupulous in pursuing it. What I did not know was whether, its own wants apart, it harboured deliberate malice. Towards me I did not think it did, or not at the moment. Towards Julia I was far less certain.

After a bit I gave it up. It seemed to me that nothing was any longer in my hands. All I could do was to leave the colonel, and Beth, and Julia herself to work things out, separately or among themselves. At some point, presumably, I should be shown what there was left for me. In the meantime I had had all I could stand. I stopped the car at a pub and drank two whiskies. It was not much, but it was better than nothing. Whatever state I was in, I was incapable of getting myself really drunk while I still had the car to drive. Later again I stopped somewhere and bought myself a meal and had half a bottle of wine with it. It was getting quite late now, and I was a long way from home. I got the maps out and made a fair fist of working out my return route. It did not in fact take me very long. If the outward journey is aimless, or even a deliberate exploration, the return journey is always quicker than you expect. All the same, they were shutting up when I drove into the yard of the King's Head, and as I came in at the door, the landlord came to meet me. He looked mildly put out. 'Oh, Mr Mackellar,' he said, 'there's been a gentleman on the phone from London for you. Several times he's rung, but of course all I could tell him was that you'd be in later.'

I stood staring at him. I could tell from the way he was looking at me that I did not look very good. I said, 'Did he leave a message?'

'No, I asked him, but he said no.'

I nodded. 'I expect he'll ring again,' I said.

'Well, no, he said he wouldn't, as a matter of fact. He said he'd write.'

I nodded again, and said good-night, and went up to my room.

CHAPTER FIFTEEN

Jimmy's letter arrived next morning, covered with extra stamps and marked Express Delivery. He must have gone to a great deal of trouble. This was the more pointed because there was not, in any practical sense, any urgency in it at all. It did not ask me to do anything. It merely told me that so far as he was concerned I could do what I liked when I liked, or go on doing nothing, so long as I left him out of it and understood that he no longer accepted any responsibility for my affairs. I suppose he just wanted to get it off his chest. Or perhaps he hoped his letter might bring me to my senses. He was not, in general, an angry or impatient man.

I did not know what in practical terms I ought to do about it. I had heard of many writers changing their agents, which meant in fact sacking one and going to another, but I had never heard of an agent sacking one of his authors, though I supposed it must happen. Not that this really worried me, because I did not at the moment want to do anything about it at all. I suppose I believed that if ever I could really get down to work again, Jimmy would probably be ready to take me on despite everything. The trouble was that I did not believe I would, and Jimmy's letter, if only because it deepened my despair, deepened my disbelief. As I stood there on that still, golden morning with Jimmy's letter in my hands, my despair touched rock bottom. I seemed to have thrown away everything for Julia, and now I seemed to have thrown away Julia too. I could not see at all what there was to look forward to.

Like most writers, at least nowadays, I was ready enough to talk fairly flippantly about my writing, but the truth is that I was desperately committed to it. I had come to it against very substantial opposition in the family, and I had made a good many important enemies and burned a good many boats on the way. On the material side this did not very much worry me, but it had its emotional side as well. My pride was involved, or at least my self-esteem. Not to put it too grandly, I very much wanted to show them. I was determined that they should at some point have to admit that the prodigal son, despite his unexpected and unfortunate preference for husks, was at least a pretty successful swineherd. And that was only part of it. Serious writing, by which I mean whole-time professional writing, is an odd business. It springs from a certain type of emotional make-up, apparently quite irrespective of any intellectual or even educational ability to write successfully. That is why the world is full of would-be, or failed, writers, in all degress of consciousness of their wish or failure. They tend to gravitate to jobs on the fringes of actual literature, and their most prominent common characteristic is their resentment, more or less conscious, of the people who have succeeded in becoming what they themselves have not. Few people, in my experience, hate writers like the average librarian. That being the way of it, anyone who has succeeded in becoming a writer – I do not mean a materially successful writer, but at least an actual public performer – very quickly gets into the frame of mind where he simply cannot imagine himself doing any other job. He may, and often does, dislike the job itself, and unless he is one of the lucky ones, he is very ready to be bitter about his failure to make much money at it or to achieve much acclaim for his performance. But he cannot give it up. The mental or emotional need which brought him to it grows stronger the more it is given way to. In the stock phrase, nothing else will satisfy him. Your unsuccessful writer starving in a garret is in general not necessarily any more admirable than your alcoholic doing the same. He is simply a man who has given way to an inborn tendency and is now hooked on it. I suppose with age or exhaustion the thing may burn itself out. It is never likely to be satisfied, because very few writers experience any emotionally satisfying sense of accomplishment. So far as their emotional needs go, the last book is dead as soon as it is written, and the next is already nagging.

When I first saw Julia in the train, I had had two books published, and I was irretrievably a writer. If someone had compelled me to choose between her and writing, I do not know what I should have done, but in fact the question would not have made sense. It could never have occurred to me that falling in love would kill my writing, any more than the alcoholic can be persuaded that his drinking will kill his marriage. Somehow or other he will manage both, but in the meantime he must drink. It is only when his wife is packing up to go that he comes face to face with what he has done. That was more or less what happened to me when I read Jimmy's letter. It was not the mere fact of losing my agent, though I was still a very inexperienced writer, and this frightened me badly. It was the fact that something had come inexorably between me and my writing, and I could not at the moment believe that I should ever write again. I felt, I suppose, like a religious man who has put himself beyond the pale and lost his faith. Jimmy's rejection of me was merely the formal act of excommunication. It was frightening in itself, but mainly it merely deepened my sense of guilt.

And there was still, as far as I could see, nothing I could do. It was no good my trying to appease Jimmy when I saw no possibility of my ever again needing his services. Equally I could not make any fresh approach to Julia until I knew the outcome of my disaster with Beth. This was the more damnable because what had happened with Beth did not

132

in any way alter what I felt about Julia. I still wanted her as desperately as ever. But it seemed to have taken out of my hands any control I had ever had over the situation, which God knows was not much. I had put myself in the power of two people, Beth in any case and Julia if she came to know what had happened, and I did not know what either of them would do. It is relatively easy, in retrospect, to set out what I felt in this sort of analytical way. At the time I had neither the wish nor the power to analyse anything. In all that golden summer weather I went about in a black night of despair, which I remember, even now, as worse than anything I have suffered since.

I say went about, but hang about would be nearer the mark. I did not go anywhere because there was nowhere to go. I was waiting for something to happen, and that meant for someone to get in touch with me. I did not know who it would be, but whoever it was, they could not find me unless I stayed where I was in Studham. Most of the time I simply sat in my room, and a bedroom in the King's Head is not the best place to sit in. I remembered a time when I had kept away from it for fear that Beth would visit me there. Now I should have welcomed a visit even from Beth, because at least it would have told me something, but Beth did not come. What did come, just about lunch-time, was a note from the colonel asking me to dinner that evening. I accepted, automatically, because there was nothing else I could do. From what he had said, I supposed Julia might be there, but whether she was or not, I supposed I should learn something. I hoped she would be, because for all my fear of the meeting, I still had little in me but the longing to see her again. But my fear was very great, and the fact that I should be meeting her in company did nothing to lessen it.

At least I had nothing more to wait for. I could get out, away from the place altogether, and come back just in time to clean myself up for the colonel's dinner. I did not want anything to eat. I just went and got the car out and drove out of Studham, running away for the second time in two days from the only thing I still knew I wanted. The curious thing is that I never, throughout this short but appalling episode, altogether lost sight of the fact that the way I was behaving was irrational to the point of lunacy. I knew perfectly well what I ought to do. I ought to write an apology to the colonel, and pack up, and pay my bill, and drive back to London, and have it out with Jimmy, and seek his help in getting started again on what I never doubted was my proper business in life. Only I could not do it. I was like a man in a nightmare, who knows all the time that it is only a nightmare, but cannot break out of it, I suppose because his terror fulfils some need in his nature below the level of his thinking mind. As Julia had said, and I wished she had not, I had drunk my proper bane, and I was helpless as long as the poison was in my system. Besides, the poison was a sweet one. So far from wanting to get rid of it, I wanted more of it if I could.

Outwardly my behaviour was unexceptionable. I even felt an unusual need to be on sympathetic terms with my fellow men in ordinary matters. I went out of my way to be friendly and cheerful with the people at the hotel and the man at the petrol pump, and my driving was almost exaggeratedly correct and considerate. All the same, I did not seek ordinary company. I avoided it as far as I could. In fact I made for the higher ground, and left my tie and jacket in the car, and walked the whole of that long hot afternoon on the tops of the hills, never meeting a soul. By the end of it I was tired and beginning to be almost light-headed with hunger and lack of sleep, because my night had been a dreadful one. But I worked to a strict time-table. I got back to the hotel with just the time I needed, and I turned in at the colonel's gate at just the time he had said in his invitation. I saw Julia's car standing in front of the house and put mine alongside it. When I went in, there were only the two of them there, the man whom I liked and who I thought liked me and the woman I loved and still believed I could bring to love me in return. There were no danger signals anywhere, and I surrendered at once to my almost desperate desire for happiness. I did not believe in my happiness as anything stable or permanent, but for the moment there was nothing to prevent it, and I took it while it was there, conscious all the time of the depths beneath. At times I even felt guilty, as if I was getting on false pretences something I had no real right to. All the same, it was the happiest evening I have ever spent.

The colonel had evidently smoothed over the fact that he and I already knew each other, and no one made any reference to it. If he was being consciously diplomatic, no hint of his diplomacy appeared on the surface, nor do I believe that, at any rate after the first, he himself remained in any way conscious of it. They were two utterly congenial people, and they seemed to feel, or at least to let me feel, that I was congenial to both of them. My love for Julia was somehow absorbed in my liking for them both. I suppose it is true, though it takes some time to discover, that you can in a way be happier with someone you love in pleasant company than you can when the two of you are alone together. It dilutes the egotism and the agonising apprehension that are so much a part of love and relates it more to the ordinary business of life. I knew then that if Beth and Charlie had not existed, I should have had nothing more to look for. I knew at the same time that both did exist and both in their different ways posed a threat to my happiness which could be lethal. But in that essentially sane company the lunatic irrationality of the threat seemed for the moment as unreal as the terror of the nightmare seems in the discovered daylight of your familiar bedroom.

When it was time to go, Julia and I got up together. We both had our cars, and there was no question of either's driving the other home, so that we made our separate goodnights to the colonel, and I think even said formal goodnights to each other. Then we got into our cars and moved off separately down the drive. But for a quarter of a mile or so our ways lay together, and by the time we came to the parting there was nothing but night and silence everywhere, and with the certainty of a pre-arranged agreement both cars stopped together.

I got out and walked over to her. I said, 'Need you go home yet? It's not late.'

'No, I don't think so. I mustn't be late, but there's plenty of time yet. Only I don't know where we can go. Do you?'

There was not a breath of wind. The stars glowed hazily from a cloudless sky, and the night smelt of hay. I said, 'Need we go anywhere?' but I knew at once that that was wrong. She looked past me out of the car window, and the night she saw was different from mine.

She said, 'I don't want to stay here. Apart from anything else, everybody knows every car by sight for miles.' I felt rebuked, as if roadside love-making was for the Beths of this world, as indeed it was, but I do not think she meant me to feel that or had any idea I did. There were just things she did not fancy doing, and it never occurred to her that I could see them in any way differently.

'I tell you what,' she said. 'Come over to Clanstead, if it won't be too far out of your way. I'll give you a drink before you go home.' She said it exactly as one man might say it to another, and yet there was nothing defensive about it, still less anything coy. She knew perfectly well what I wanted, and was disposed up to a point to grant it. It was just that she lacked altogether the language of love or any of the small vulgarisms that love takes refuge in. I hated the idea of Windbarrow, I mean the house itself, at night, but could not say so. Perhaps after all when we got there, and the two cars were safely off the road, she would walk out with me somewhere and not insist on my going into that damned house, with its silence and its shut doors and the listening gallery overhead. Anyway, I had to take a chance on it.

'All right,' I said, 'you lead on and I'll follow.' I went back to my car, and presently she started hers and moved off, and I drove after her. All I could see of her was the red tail-lights of the car, and I felt utterly cut off from her. There are few things more insulated from each other than two cars moving on a road at night. She drove as I knew she would, and as I had seen the colonel drive, with a sort of unhurried efficiency, which never appeared to cut any corners, but in those lanes took a great deal of keeping up with. But I am sure that the idea of setting a pace never occurred to her. Even with someone driving behind and following every manoeuvre, she drove exactly as she would on an empty road, and there are very few people who can do that.

She swung into the Windbarrow gate at last, and I swung in and parked alongside her, as I had earlier at the Grange. We switched off lights and engines at once, and the cars made very little noise on the soft gravel. I do not think anyone in the house would have known of our arrival unless they were looking for it. There were no signs of life anywhere. I could see some faint lights showing indirectly from upstairs windows, but on the ground floor there were no lights at all. She got out of her car and stood for a moment looking up at the house. Then she turned and shut the door of the car, and I noticed that she did it very quietly. I did the same, and for a moment we stood there peering at each other in the sweet-scented gloom. Then she came round to where I was standing and took me by the hand. 'Come on,' she said. She did not whisper, but her voice was as small and quiet as ever.

For my part I did whisper. That was what the damned

place made me feel like I said, 'Must we go in? Can't we stay outside?'

She shook her head and closed her fingers slightly on my hand, and I walked with her across the gravel to the front door. She opened it with a latchkey. It all seemed to make very little noise, but I still could not make out whether she was being deliberately quiet or not. I know I was. There was a single light burning in the hall, and the house was completely silent. We went across to the door of her working room. I think I had been in it before, but now that I had seen the colonel's room at Uppishley, the likeness struck me at once. The colonel's room lacked aggressive masculinity, and Julia's was more masculine than you would expect. The result was the same combination of practicality and elegance. She switched on a standard lamp and a lamp on the desk. 'Wait here, will you?' she said. 'I shan't be a moment.' She went out and shut the door behind her, and I was left standing there in the absolute silence. At least the curtains were drawn, and I did not feel myself overlooked from outside. I do not know how long she was away. It cannot have been very long, because I do not remember doing anything special. I just stood there, taking in the room. She came in again as quietly as she had gone out and shut the door behind her.

I felt so clearly that she had been on some sort of tour of inspection that I said, 'All well?'

She nodded. 'Charlie's asleep,' she said. 'Beth's out. I don't think she'll be in just yet.'

'Shall we hear her if she does come?'

'Not necessarily. She usually leaves her car at the back and comes in that way. But she wouldn't come in here.'

I nodded and went straight across to her, where she stood with her back to the door. She knew exactly what she was about. Her eyes held mine as I came towards her, but the watchful look had gone, and her face was utterly peaceful. Above all, she waited, neither drawing in on

138

herself nor coming to meet me. Just at the last moment her hands came up, and I went into her arms like a ship going into harbour. It was a long kiss, but very gentle. Then she took her mouth from mine and said, 'Ian, what's the matter?'

I could not believe at that moment that anything was the matter anywhere, the whole pattern of my life had changed so. I think I frowned at her a little. There was no conscious prevarication in it. The state I had been in only those few hours before seemed infinitely remote, and I really could not understand. 'When?' I said.

She said, 'This evening. When you came to the Grange. You looked dreadful.'

I nodded. I remembered it all now, but it did not seem to belong to me any more, like the terrible things you can remember doing in childhood. She said, 'Was it anything to do with Beth?'

Even now there was no panic in me, because the moment for panic had already passed, and here we still were, she and I, in each other's arms. All the same I did not answer her directly. I said, 'Why Beth?'

She was not looking at me now. 'I don't know,' she said. 'Just the way she's been going on. I know her very well.' She seemed to be speaking almost to herself, as if Beth was a private problem of hers in which I was in no way involved.

I waited, holding her where she was, until she looked at me again. I was determined to be involved. I knew there was no other way. When she raised her eyes, I said, 'Yes. It was Beth. She—', but her arms tightened on me suddenly.

'No,' she said, 'no, it doesn't matter. Only I had to know. It doesn't matter, does it?'

I said, 'Nothing matters, only—', but she stopped me again.

She said, 'No, all right.' We were back to our lovers'

shorthand. After a bit she said, 'It's Charlie really, isn't it?'

'I think so, yes.'

'Can't you get on with him?'

The thing had come sooner than I had expected, but even so it had to be faced. I said, 'He doesn't like me.'

Her face was full of distress now, but there was nothing I could do to help her or to help myself. She said, 'He does, Ian, really he does. He's fond of you. I told you.'

I shook my head at her. I did not dare say anything. I loved her, looking down at her unhappy face like that, more than I had ever yet, but I shook my head at her, because there was nothing else I could do. She said, 'But I can't—' She stopped, staring up at me, and I bent my face down to hers.

'You must,' I said. I kissed her hard. I was forcing the pace now, and for a moment I thought she would give way, but she did not. After a little she pushed me away from her and stood there, with her eyes down, considering the thing in absolute silence and immobility, as if I was not there at all. We were still standing just inside the door.

Then she said, 'You'd better go now.' She still seemed to be speaking from some enormous distance. I let go of her altogether. I knew she did not want to be touched.

I said, 'All right.' I reached past her and put my hand on the handle of the door. Just for a moment she put a hand on my arm, but then she took it away again, and I opened the door and went out into the hall. I walked across to the front door and opened that too. She had followed me, and we stood there, with me just outside the door and her just inside it, wondering if there was anything more we could say to each other.

It was a very small sound, but we both heard it. Somewhere upstairs a door clicked shut. Her head went up, and we both listened, but there was nothing more at all.

Then she lifted a finger to her lips. I nodded and turned away, and she shut the door, very quietly, behind me.

CHAPTER SIXTEEN

It was hotter than ever next day, and the haze was denser, blurring the outlines of things quite close at hand. In fact it was the last day of the hot weather, as it was of so much else. The thing had run its course, and the break was coming. The first person I saw was Beth, and she was the last person I expected to see. I do not know why, when I had been half expecting her the day before. I suppose it was because she no longer seemed to constitute a threat. She sailed in, that last brilliant morning, looking like Perdita dressed for the party, except that her flowers were not wild ones in her arms, but psychedelic ones printed on what there was of her dress. She made quite a stir at the King's Head, though they must have been used to her, and I was almost glad to see her myself. This was because I was no longer afraid of her, but she did not know that, and it puzzled her a little.

She said, 'It's going to be a scorching day. Are you coming to Grainger's?'

I said, 'Me and who else?'

I smiled at her cheerfully, and she said, 'Oh. Well, Charlie, I suppose. He's sure to want to swim.'

'All right,' I said. 'You go down in your own time, and I'll follow presently.'

She looked at me. She was unsure of me now altogether.

She said, 'You really will come?'

What I really wanted was to know what time she had got in the night before, but I did not feel up to asking her direct. I thought it might perhaps emerge presently. All I said was, 'I will, really,' and she took herself off, still not knowing quite what to make of me.

I hung about for a bit after she had gone, because I wanted to make sure that she and Charlie had left the house before I got there. On the other hand, if I was going to see Julia, which of course was what I was hoping to do, it would be better not to leave it too late. In the end I gave Beth half an hour's start and then went and got the car out. I was in fact too late to see Julia. At any rate, she was no longer at Windbarrow when I got there, though for all I knew she might have been out and away even before Beth had appeared at Studham. There was nothing left for it but to walk down the path to Grainger's. But I thought I would go cautiously, and make sure they were both there before I committed myself to joining them. They were both, for different reasons and in their very different ways, people I did not want to find myself alone with. I also thought that later, when they left the pool, I might stay there, or perhaps double back to it if I found I had to leave when they did, in the hope that Julia might come down later on her own. With the day as it was, she would surely want to come some time. The one thing I would not in any circumstances let myself do was sleep by the pool.

I picked my way down the path in the stifling heat, liking the thing and the place less and less the farther I went. I went on because I had told Beth I would, and it was important that I should keep on even terms with her, and indeed perhaps at some point have the whole thing out with her. At all events, the one thing I could not afford was to seem to run away from her, even if it would not be only or even mainly her I was running away from.

Before I got too near the pool I turned off the path and

took a line I had never followed before, up the west side of the valley. I was still making for the pool, but at a higher level, so that instead of emerging on to the grass bank, I came out from among the trees and found myself looking down on to the pool from above. The difference in height was not much. I suppose I was a foot or two higher than the top of the dam. I had heard their voices while I was still in the trees, and now I saw Charlie and Beth both in the water, swimming about in it in that unbelievably easy way they had. I think it was really only because they were both in all circumstances extraordinarily graceful movers, but the effect was definitely uncanny, as if they really were amphibious creatures. I was reminded at once of my dream. Of course the picture was very different, but I knew, in the way you sometimes do, that this was what my dream had been about. Anyone who has thought about it knows, without theorising about it, that you can sometimes dream of things that have not yet happened. In my dream I had seen only one of them, but I had known all along that they were both there.

However, this was the thing I had wanted to make sure of. I stood and watched them for a moment or two, and then went back into the trees. They had neither of them seen me. I went back the way I had come and rejoined the path where I had left it. Then I went on down it in my deliberately casual walk, swinging my swimming things in my hand, until I came out on to the grass bank. They were both still in the water. Beth's towel was spread on the grass. I had never seen Charlie with a towel at all. I supposed he must use one to dry himself, but I had a feeling that the water ran off his golden skin naturally, as if he had scales.

They saw me as I came down to the edge of the water. Beth waved and called to me, and then turned over and swam towards the bank at my feet. Charlie did not make any sign, but he was watching me, with his eyes just above the surface of the water. As so often happened when the three of us were together, he seemed to slip back into a world of his own, so that Beth at least behaved almost as if he was not there. I could never make out whether this was Beth's doing or his, or whether it was something they did by mutual agreement. Whether Charlie liked it I also did not know, but that was how it was. One moment there were the two of them together without me, and the next there were Beth and I together, and Charlie, although physically present, seemed to have left us to ourselves. Beth said, 'It's marvellous. Come on in.'

'I will,' I said, 'but no hurry. I'll go and change, anyhow.' I walked up on to the dam and over the bridge to the changing place. I was never out of earshot, but I did not hear them say anything to each other at all, not once they knew I was there, and yet when I had been coming down to the pool, I had heard their voices all the time. It gave me an odd feeling of exclusion, rather like the feeling when you come into a room full of people talking among themselves, and the conversation stops, and you do not know at all what it was they were talking about before you came in. I got into my trunks and went back along the dam to the grass bank, taking my towel with me. Beth was out now, sitting on her spread towel and sunning herself. Charlie was still in the water. I spread my towel on the grass and sat down beside her. I remembered, of course, what had happened the last time we had been there, but I had the feeling that she was more conscious of it than I was. Julia had told me it did not matter, and I had told her it did not matter, and that seemed to be the way of it. The one certain thing, to me at least, was that it would never happen again. But I did not yet know whether Beth knew this or not.

She said, 'You're an unexpected sort of person, aren't you?'

'Am I?' I said. 'I thought I always did the obvious thing.

You were the one who was unexpected. I was asleep. I wasn't expecting anyone. How long had you been there, in fact?'

'Me? I was changing, and I saw you come down the path. So I just watched you.'

'Yes. You're always watching people, aren't you? You and Charlie. Was Charlie there too?'

I do not think I had ever succeeded in upsetting her before, but this did. She actually flushed a little. 'Of course not,' she said. 'If you'd gone in the water, I expect I'd have joined you, but you didn't. You just lay down here, and presently I realised you'd gone to sleep. That's very provoking, you know. There's a great temptation to look at people when they're asleep. They look so different. So I came over to have a good look at you. And then you woke up, and one thing sort of led to another.'

'It did indeed. But it won't any more. That's really what I wanted to tell you.'

'No?' she said. 'I wonder.'

'No,' I said. 'Just a flash in the pan.'

'I see. A pity, all the same. It was quite a flash.'

'Look,' I said, 'your life must be a practically continuous firework display. Only leave me out of it in future.'

'All right,' she said. 'Only watch where you sleep.'

'I will,' I said, and then I turned and saw Charlie watching us from the edge of the water. He must have come up silently under the bank, and now he hung there, with his arms anchored on the grass verge and his head resting on them, looking at us. He was not hiding or anything. He just hung there, fully in view once you looked, but watching us with a fixed unembarrassed attention, as if he was in fact looking out of some hidden vantage point. He was only a few yards from us. I had had the feeling often enough that he was not really there when I could see him in front of me, but I had always thought it was he who was in some way unaware of my existence. Now I knew he was

145

watching me, but I felt he was assuming my unawareness of him, as if in his own mind he had put on a cloak of invisibility. It only lasted a moment, but it was so disturbing that I had an immediate urge to establish contact with him, just as, if you find a child hiding and believing itself still hidden, you feel bound to let it know you have seen it. I said, 'Hullo, Charlie. What's it like? As cold as ever?' It was the sort of pointless thing you do say, but I had to say something.

His eyes changed, it was impossible to say how, but as if he was somehow coming into focus. He smiled his slow, detached smile, which did not expect you to know what it was he was really smiling at. 'I don't find it cold,' he said. There was never anything wrong with his voice. It was as normal as Beth's, with all the usual conversational tones in it. 'You coming in?'

I said again, 'Presently.' I had no intention of going into the water while he was there. He nodded, still smiling, and his head disappeared under the bank. I did not hear a sound, but a moment or two later I saw him swimming on the far side of the pool.

Beth said, 'We'll have to be going up to the house soon.' It startled me, because I had forgotten she was there. My mind was entirely concentrated on Charlie. It seemed impossible for the three of us to remain simultaneously conscious of each other's presence. I turned and looked at her, but she was not looking at me at all. She was flat on her back on the towel, looking up at the sky through half-closed eyes. After a bit she turned her head sideways and said, 'Are you going in, in fact?'

'Not yet.' For a moment she looked at me, still through half-closed lids. Then she gave a sort of nod and turned her face to the sky again. I lay down myself, with the last of that golden June heat soaking into me and complete silence everywhere. It should have been utterly peaceful, but it was not. Beth lay beside me on the grass, and somewhere Charlie moved silently about the pool. They had both asked me if I was going into the water, and I had told both of them that I was not going in yet, and now Beth had said that they must go up to the house soon. The question of time had been raised and left unanswered. I did not want it asked direct, because I did not want to answer it. I knew myself that I was not going in until they had gone, but I did not want to say so. I wanted them just to take themselves off, leaving me where I was, but I could not be certain what either of them would do, and I felt the tension growing. For all I knew, it might be entirely in my own mind, but I did not think so, because that kind of mental unease, like the physical tension between two people, is never really one-sided. Come to that, it might be three-sided. Beth might be waiting on Charlie, and Charlie on Beth, as much as I was waiting on them and they on me. I was never sure what the relation was between them. At times they seemed virtually one person, as identical twins do, and at others they seemed to belong to different worlds. The trouble was that the thing was constantly changing, so that you never knew where you were with them. At the moment the fact that Beth and I never moved a muscle and Charlie could neither be seen nor heard was only making it worse. I felt pinned down, so that I myself dared not move. I think I was actually trying to hold my breath.

It was Beth who made the move at last. I heard her sit up, and I knew that she turned and looked at me, but I did not look at her. Then she called 'Charlie!' and he answered at once from somewhere quite close at hand. The voices were very much alike, and both sounded perfectly ordinary. The tension snapped, and I felt an enormous relief flooding over me. All the same, I was not going to move yet. Beth said, 'Time we were going,' and again Charlie answered her. I could not hear what he said. I was still flat on the grass, and I think he must have been down under the bank, but it still sounded quite ordinary. It was

147

only when Beth got up that I moved at all. I rolled over on my face and looked up at her.

'Are you going?' I said, and she nodded quite briskly.

'Yes,' she said, 'time we were off. Come on, Charlie.'

She walked across to the dam, and a moment later I saw Charlie follow her. At the top they separated, Beth going straight over the top and Charlie along the dam and over the bridge, until he too disappeared. I did not turn on to my back again. I lay there on my side, facing the dam, waiting for them to re-appear. They were suddenly two ordinary people again, and I wondered whether all the tensions between us were not entirely of my creating. All the same, I could hardly wait for them to go.

They appeared, in fact, almost simultaneously on top of the dam and came down on to the grass together. They did not say anything, either to me or to each other, but they both seemed quite cheerful. They passed me, Beth in front of me and Charlie behind, as I sat on the grass, and went off up the path towards the house. I still did not go into the water, not at once. I sat there staring at it, with my hands clasped round my knees. I thought that Charlie had one of his appointments with Julia at about this time. I had never been sure of the exact timing of his day, but I knew that it was at about this time of the morning. I wondered if he would tell her that I was down at the pool. I was fairly certain that Beth would not, even if she saw her, but with Charlie I was never sure of anything. Perhaps, on a day like this, Julia would come down anyhow.

I roused myself at last. I got to my feet and walked over to the edge of the water, leaving my towel where it was on the grass. The air was breathless, and there was not a sound anywhere. Even in my trunks I was starting to sweat, and the water looked suddenly desirable. I walked along almost to the bottom of the dam and then went off in a long flat dive, heading for the middle of the pool.

For the first time that I could remember, the feel of the water closing over me was unmixed pleasure. I swam out lazily into the middle, and then turned on my back and floated with my arms spread sideways, as I had twice seen Julia floating. For the first time and the last time in that place I felt utterly at peace. Presently I turned on my face and swam again, looking down into the amber depths under me. It was while I was swimming like that that I felt the shock as something hit the water on the far side of the pool. I whipped my face out of the water and spun round to look.

Charlie was swimming towards me, for once with his face well out of the water. His eyes were wide open and looked startlingly blue, and there was a cheerful, excited smile on his face. 'I've come back,' he said, and came on straight towards me.

CHAPTER SEVENTEEN

I shall never know what, at that moment, he really had in his mind. His smile was so boyish and compelling that I know I smiled back at him, and I do not think that at that stage I was actually afraid. What I did feel was the same physical repulsion I had felt before. I did not want him to touch me, least of all in the water, where I felt most clearly that he was strange flesh, and where I was myself almost without clothes. If there was fear, it was the sort of instinctive fear you feel of a harmless water-snake, not what you feel of a shark. That sort of fear came later.

He swam straight for me and grappled with me. It was

not very serious grappling, the sort of horseplay I had seen many times between him and Beth, and now he was actually laughing, a small continuous giggle. I still did not want him to touch me. I pushed him off, and I think splashed water in his face, but of course it was like splashing water at an amphibian. If he did not actually breathe it, it did not stop him breathing the air he needed. He was between me and the nearest point of the bank, and what I wanted above all was to get out of the water as soon as possible. I put out my strength, forcing him backwards a little, but I soon found that in the water my greater strength counted for little and my greater weight for nothing at all. I did not want to hit him, as I had once before. I was nowhere near that point of desperation yet. I was still repelled, but in a sort of way embarrassed by my repulsion, so that I wanted to conceal it if I could. All the same, I had not managed to get much nearer the bank.

I was wondering what to do next when he suddenly let go of me and turned sideways and dived. I struck out hard for the bank. I knew he was somewhere in the water underneath me, and for the first time a touch of real fear, a sort of horror, took hold of me, and I swam as if for my life. The next moment he had got hold of one of my legs. Only one, thank God. I kicked out furiously with the other, and caught him quite hard somewhere, but I did not know where. At any rate, he let go for the moment, and I swam on a few more strokes. I had got quite close to the bank before he tackled me again.

He had still not come up for air, and I could not believe that, even with his unnatural ability to hold his breath, he could stay under much longer, not putting out the amount of energy he was. I myself gulped in all the air I could. I did it only just in time, because a moment later he had me under. This time he simply wrapped his arms round me somewhere between the waist and the knees and pulled me straight under. This is the classic way of drowning anyone, much practised, if the books are to be believed, by husbands on unsuspecting wives. I do not know whether at this stage he meant to drown me, but even if he did, two things were against him. First, I was not unsuspecting, but went under with a clear knowledge of what I was up against and my lungs as full of air as I could get them. Second and more important, we were too close to the bank. There was enough water even here to drown in, but not really enough for one person, working under water, to drag another vertically under. As I say, my head went under, but never very far and not for long. I struggled with my legs instinctively, and I think Charlie himself must have hit bottom, because the downward drag stopped abruptly, and I began, much too slowly but unmistakably, to surface again. Soon after that the inevitable happened. Charlie simply let go and came up for air, and we got our heads out at very much the same moment, facing each other and a few yards apart.

I suppose that was the decisive moment, when the thing might have gone either way. Charlie might have got away with being a dangerously violent joker, given to ducking people for the laugh of it, and I might have come out of it as a sensible adult, too big to be frightened by such fooling and too level-headed to be provoked by it. It does not seem worth arguing, now, whose fault it was that it did not finish that way. If Charlie had kept his mouth shut or I had kept my temper, it might have, but we did not. I suppose he was angry that he had not got the better of me. What that would have involved I do not know, and I doubt if he knew himself, but evidently he was not satisfied. We were now both gasping for air, but the look on his face was very different. I do not think he would have laughed even if he had had any spare breath to laugh with. His eyes glared, and the shape of his mouth was very ugly. He took a breath and said, 'For Christ's sake, why can't you bugger off and leave us in peace? You've had Beth. I tell you, you're not having Jule.'

151

The voice was high and almost childish, and went with the silly obscenity, and I think if he had left Julia out of it, I might still have let it go. But I knew now. I knew he was going to keep his hold on Julia if he could, and I knew too much about the pair of them now to have much doubt that he could if he chose. All my bottled up anger and frustration came to the surface, and above all my sense of lunatic unfairness of the whole thing. I said, 'You poor little crackpot, it's time you were shut up.' Then I turned and swam to the bank.

I was out of the water and had my hands on the grass when he came at me from behind and got his arms round me under the armpits. It was what I had seen him do to Beth, but that had been only horseplay. Now he was in earnest. We went back into the water with a tremendous splash, both on our backs and with me half on top of him. My face went under, and this time I was not ready for it. I swallowed a lot of water and came up choking for air, and by the time I could get my breath properly I realised what he was up to.

He was dragging me out into the middle of the pool. He had an astonishing power of propulsion in the water. He would have made a marvellous life-saver, but at the moment it was not saving life he had in mind. We neither of us said anything more after that. We fought silently, saving our breath, because it was breath we were fighting for. For the moment I let myself go with him. The only thing I could not let him do was keep me on my back, because like that I was completely helpless. I took a couple of deep breaths while we went on surging across the pool. Then I put up both hands to one of his and broke its grip on me. I needed both hands for it, but I managed it. As his hand slipped off me, I rolled convulsively sideways, and the next moment we were facing each other again, both treading water, both out of breath and clear out in the middle of that damned pool.

152

He came at me at once, and this time he tried a new form of attack. I had seen it done often before, but never quite like this. The principle of the thing is simple. Nearly submerged bodies have little weight, but once most of a body is out of the water, it weighs normally, and as such makes a burden which a swimming man cannot possibly sustain. So you get your hands on the other man's shoulders and heave yourself out of the water, getting your weight on top of him, and down he goes. He cannot possibly do anything else. If you can get him down far enough, you can get your feet on him and tread him under, and then he is really in trouble. As I say, I had seen this way of ducking people before, and probably had it done to me in a light-hearted sort of way, but I had forgotten its appalling effectiveness, especially as Charlie did it. He came surging up to me and got his hands on my shoulders before I knew what he was at, and then he shot straight up into the air, using his legs on the water and using his arms on me as if I was a vaulting horse. He was not a heavy man, but the human body is surprisingly dense, as anyone knows who has tried dandling even a fair-sized baby, if people dandle babies these days, which I doubt. Charlie got almost his whole weight out of the water and bearing directly on my shoulders. I just went down like a stone, and again I was not ready for it.

The water came bursting into my nose and mouth, and I had little reserve air in my lungs to blow it out again. I held my breath instinctively, but I did not think I could hold it very long, and I kept going down and down, and out here there was no bottom at any sort of a depth that was likely to be of any interest to me. I think if Charlie had kept his hands on me and dived after me, he would have had me. Somewhere down in that cold yellow water I should have let my breath go, and there would have been nothing but water to take its place. As it was, he tried using his feet, and that saved me. For one thing he did not

153

manage to get them squarely on to me, and first one and then the other slipped off. For another, even if you get someone down in that way, you cannot get him further down than your height, and in Charlie's case this was not all that far. Once I was free of him and coming up again, I did not really have very far to come, and I got my head out just before my lungs gave up the struggle and threw their useless air out. Even so, I was pretty far gone. I just kicked about wildly on the surface, choking and utterly panic-stricken, and I saw Charlie's face in front of me, watching me with a smile on his mouth and murder in his eyes. I think I tried to scream, and this no doubt added to his enjoyment.

It must have been his enjoyment that did for him. He held off for a few moments while I backed desperately away from him, and then just as he started to come at me again, my foot touched something solid under water. First one foot touched it and then the other. They talk of a drowning man clutching at a straw, but nobody ever used his hands with as much instinctive desperation as I used my feet. I felt for it and found it and got my feet squarely on it before I even clearly understood that I was standing, with my head just clear of the water, on the flat top of Old Mole.

Charlie was on me again a second later, but it was a second too late. He did what he had done before, getting his hands on my shoulders and heaving himself up on me, but this time my body stood up rigidly under his weight, and I no longer wasted my arms flailing uselessly at the water. As the front of his body went up past my face, I hit it as hard as I could, first with one hand and then with the other. I cannot have hit him very hard, and they were no more than the short jabs of in-fighting, but one at least must have caught him where it mattered and knocked the breath out of him. He let go his grip and simply slithered straight down in front of me, and for a second we were face to face, almost touching, but now his face had nothing in it but a sort of horrified surprise. I reached out, still just balanced on that uncouth pinnacle of rock, and got hold of his head and pushed it under.

I suppose as much as anything it was the shock that finished him, though perhaps he was in any case more exhausted than in my desperation I had allowed for. He came up again slowly, with his eyes almost shut and his mouth open, choking, with the water running out of it. I could not stand the sight of him. I do not think there was anything left in me but a sort of horrified repulsion. I lunged forward at him, and this time my feet slipped off the rock and I was afloat again, but now I did not mind. I was over him, treading his almost unresisting body down into the water under me, when I suddenly found that, Charlie or no Charlie, I could not stay afloat much longer. I left him and swam blindly for the bank.

I only just got there. I went under once, but came up again, and now the bank was quite close, and I put out the last of my strength and got a hand to it. I could not climb it, not at first. I just clung to it with both hands, fighting to get my breath back and stop myself from slipping back into that damned water. After a bit I started trying to climb out, and at the second attempt I made it. I crawled a little way over the warm blessed grass, and then stopped and turned my head. He was still out in the middle of the pool, floating on the surface now, but floating face-down. Then my arms went from under me, and I too went flat on my face.

I do not know how long I lay there. I only know that after a bit I heard Julia's voice. She was coming down the path, calling. She called, 'Charlie! Beth! Where are you?', exactly as she had that first morning.

CHAPTER EIGHTEEN

The coroner found death by misadventure. There was not much else he could do. I dealt very circumspectly with Charlie in my evidence, and even more circumspectly with myself. The doctor was careful, too, but he could not keep all the cats in the bag. He talked of extreme excitability calling for regular sedation, and admitted that if the sedation was omitted or delayed, the excitability might result in some degree of physical violence. All this fitted in very well with my story of horseplay ending in disaster, and nearly double disaster at that. My evidence was true as far as it went, but it did not go quite far enough. I did not see fit to mention Old Mole. Nobody in court knew about Old Mole, and the few people who did had evidently not thought of it as relevant.

I went to the court with the colonel and came away with him after it was over. I had not seen Julia since I had helped her get Charlie's body out of the pool. As we were driving away, the colonel said, 'As well as could be expected, I think. What happened, in fact? He went for you I suppose?'

'I'm afraid so,' I said. 'He came back specially. That was why he gave Beth the slip. If he really did, that is. What he actually had in mind I don't know. To start with, I mean. By the end he was out to drown me, and damned nearly did. He was far better in the water than I was. On land I could have dealt with him, but I couldn't get there. He wouldn't let me.'

The colonel nodded. 'Julia's taking it very hard,' he said.

'It will take her some time to get over it. I don't know what to advise you, except to leave her alone. I'm very sorry, but there it is. You'll be going back to London, I imagine?'

'Yes,' I said. I had already decided on that. I knew I could do no good there. What I had not known was whether I should see Julia again before I left. From what the colonel had said, it sounded as though I should not.

He said again, 'Well, I'm sorry. Keep in touch, will you? With me, I mean. Things may straighten themselves out.'

'I will,' I said. He dropped me at the King's Head, and we said good-bye, though not very cheerfully. I have not seen him since.

It was the middle of the afternoon before I found myself ready to go. The weather had broken completely in a series of thunder storms. It was not cold, and there was no wind at all, but everything was heavy with wet, and the sky was dark as pitch. I do not know what made me do it, but I drove off into the side lane, left the car in the usual place and walked up to the barrow. I do not think I had anything more in mind than to have a last look at the place, but when I got there, I saw Julia walking up the hill towards me. It was just what she might do, of course, with things as they were, but I had not consciously thought of that. She had not seen me. I went back into the ditch, and tried to make up my mind. If she was not going to see me, I had not got very long to do it, and I was in no mood for constructive thinking. In the end I just waited and let her find me. She did not even seem very surprised to see me. She looked desperately unhappy, but she came up to me and faced me squarely. We did not touch each other. She said, 'Are you going?'

I said, 'Yes,' and she nodded but did not say anything.

'Shall I see you again?' I said.

'I don't know,' she said. 'I shouldn't think so.' She said it not as if she was announcing a decision, but as if she

157

was simply facing a fact. There was no indignation in it. She sounded utterly listless.

I said, 'That's not fair to either of us.'

'I don't think fairness comes into it. It's a question of what's possible. For me, anyhow. Whatever was wrong with Charlie, he was my brother, and I loved him and felt responsible for him, and he was fond of you, and you let him drown.' She put out a hand and caught my arm, almost shaking it. She said, 'Why, Ian, why, except that you felt he got in your way?'

'I was within an inch of drowning myself. You know that. You know the state I was in when you found me. I only just got ashore. Charlie was better in the water than I was.'

She said, 'Do you think I haven't thought of that?' She looked at me and I looked at her and could find nothing more to say. I turned and walked up on to the side of the ditch. There was no one to hide from now. She said, 'Ian, what are you going to do?'

I turned again and looked down at her. 'I don't know,' I said. 'Wait for you, I suppose.'

She shook her head but did not say anything, and I turned for the last time and walked away from her up the slope of the hill.

That was all some time back. No one has telephoned yet. I have been meaning to telephone Jimmy, but there does not seem to be much I can say to him. I was afraid at first it might be Beth who telephoned. Beth is the only person who actually saw me stand on Old Mole, and she might remember. But Beth has not telephoned either.

P. M. HUBBARD

P. M. Hubbard was educated at Oxford, where he won the Newdigate Prize for English Verse in 1933. From 1934 to 1947 he served in the Indian Civil Service and upon its disbandment returned to England to work for the British Council in London. In 1951 he resigned to free lance as a writer. Later he was employed as deputy director of an industrial organization, but again resigned to earn his living writing. Three of his previous suspense novels have been selections of the Detective Book Club; one, *The Dancing Man,* of the Mystery Guild.